DAMAGE DONE BY
THE STORM

Stories by

JACK HODGINS

DAMAGE DONE BY
THE STORM

BY JACK HODGINS

FICTION

Spit Delaney's Island
The Invention of the World
The Resurrection of Joseph Bourne
The Barclay Family Theatre
The Honorary Patron
The Macken Charm
Broken Ground
Distance
Damage Done By The Storm

FOR CHILDREN

Left Behind in Squabble Bay

NON-FICTION

A Passion for Narrative: A Guide for Writing Fiction

DAMAGE DONE BY
THE STORM

stories by

JACK HODGINS

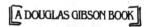

A DOUGLAS GIBSON BOOK

M&S

National Library of Canada Cataloguing in Publication

Hodgins, Jack, 1938-
Damage done by the storm : stories / by Jack Hodgins.

"A Douglas Gibson book".
ISBN 0-7710-4152-7

I. Title.

PS8565.O3D34 2004   C813'.54   C2004-902389-6

We acknowledge the financial support of the Government of Canada through the Book Publishing Industry Development Program and that of the Government of Ontario through the Ontario Media Development Corporation's Ontario Book Initiative. We further acknowledge the support of the Canada Council for the Arts and the Ontario Arts Council for our publishing program.

Some of these stories were previously published in slightly altered form. "Astonishing the Blind" was commissioned by CBC Radio and published in *Story*. "Over Here" was published in *Prism: international*. "Balance" was published in both *Paris Transcontinental* and *Story*. "Galleries" was published in *Meanjin*. "Promise" was published in the *Victoria Times Colonist*. "The Crossing" was published in *Vancouver Magazine*

The characters and events in these stories are fictitious.

Book design by Terri Nimmo
Typeset in Goudy by M&S, Toronto
Printed and bound in Canada
This book is printed on acid-free paper that is
100% ancient forest friendly (100% post-consumer recycled).

A Douglas Gibson Book

McClelland & Stewart Ltd.
The Canadian Publishers
481 University Avenue
Toronto, Ontario
M5G 2E9
www.mcclelland.com

1 2 3 4 5   08 07 06 05 04

For Doris Child

CONTENTS

BALANCE

I know what he wants. He thinks there is something wrong. The feet have been coming back, my workmanship has been slipping. "Is there something on your mind?" he will say, when he has closed the door so that the others can't hear. "Are there problems in your life?" He will lower his voice, and sound genuinely interested, so that I won't take offence. "You're the best person we've ever had on Stage Two, but something must be wrong."

He won't fire me. It takes too long to train someone to become as skilled as I am at this job. He will have to be satisfied to hear that I've had a few bad days. It happens.

I don't know what it is about me that causes him to speak in that tone. It is as though he believes he is speaking to someone who might burst into tears, or explode in a terrible tantrum. This sort of thing has happened all my life. My father would grab my brother right up out of his act of teasing the dog and start paddling him on the spot, hollering all the while. But if I threw a shoe across the room because its laces refused to unknot, he would guide me firmly into another room, close the door, and sit down to look me sadly in the face. "What's the matter with you now? You know better than that. Do you think the lace will untie itself if you throw it?" Greg Morrison, who is the manager here at

I

Stanford Orthotics, can be brutal when he is displeased with the others – "Smarten up, for chrissake, willya? This is a piece of shit." But with me he uses very much the same tone as my father did. It is as though the whole world knows how easy it is to make me ashamed.

When they promoted me to Stage Two, it was to replace a fellow who'd been laid off because so many of his feet were sent back. He was fast but not very good. At first I was lucky if I managed to complete just two in a shift. It took me a month – standing eight hours every day at my bench – but eventually I was completing sixteen to twenty a shift without any failures. "You're a real artist," Morrison said – his best compliment. He has repeated it often. It gives him pleasure to think that the painters and sculptors and failed architecture students he hires are doing a job that has at least a little in common with their artistic ambitions. "I like to watch your face when you work," he will say to me. "You could be Michelangelo grappling with David."

I wouldn't know about that. My job at Stage Two is to take the brown plaster casts that are made in Stage One from the moulds sent in by doctors all across the country – dainty feet, ugly feet, children's feet – and to measure them, line them up, centre them, weigh them, find where the imperfections are, and then, with white plaster, build whatever is needed to establish a perfect balance. My white additions, then, become models for the plastic inserts created in the next room. I like to think I have done my part to ease limps, eliminate backaches, and cut down on the strained calf muscles for half the people I pass on the street.

Sometimes I could believe that every foot in the country has passed through my hands in the three years I've worked here. They pile up by the hundreds in the room behind me. Fallen arches, twisted toes, inadequate heels. It is a peculiar thing, to realize how many people are operating at a painful tilt. Mr. Peter McConnell of Corner Brook, Newfoundland, should be walking straight as a perfect soldier now. Alice Degrout of Red Deer, Alberta, can – if she walks slowly – disguise the fact that her right foot has been deprived of its natural heel. When I first worked at Stage One, I could not help but notice that every foot had a name, a physician, and an address attached. It was always a surprise to discover that an enormous, twisted foot that you could imagine belonging to some hairy Sasquatch in the Coast Mountain Range was actually the possession of a Bambi Duchamp, whose doctor kept an office in Sainte-Agathe. I have a great deal of affection for Bambi Duchamp, who is a pretty woman, I imagine, in her Sainte-Agathe apartment, suffering torments of self-consciousness about her gigantic feet, despairing of ever finding shoes that will hide her imperfection from a merciless world. I have a great deal of affection for all those who spend a little time at my workbench and then pass on. When I think of them, I imagine that all their aches and limps and malformations have been deposited with the plaster casts in the storage room behind me, and that they have all gone on to live strong and fulfilling lives in a state of confident balance.

Sometimes, quite unexpectedly and in the most unlikely moments, I believe that I can feel in my hand the memory of a certain foot it has held. I can be riding in the bus, heading for work, and will feel all at once a particular shape in my palm. Daisy Martin, I will think. Swift Current, Saskatchewan. And blush, so help me, at the thought. It is as though I can feel the very warmth of Daisy Martin's flesh. More than that, in such moments I sense that I have established some sort of relationship

with its owner, though we have never met. I believe that if Daisy
Martin of Swift Current were to drop in at the shop I would recognize her immediately. It is a peculiar thing, but consider how
very few feet a person will ever hold in his hands. And how inti-
mate is the connection when you do – a wife's, a lover's, a child's.
Sometimes my fingers will burn with the secrets they have
somehow learned but haven't known how to tell me. There have
been times when I have worked for most of an hour with the
small foot of a child, say, holding it, turning it, stroking it with my
blade, so that when it is time to pass it on I do so as if I were
parting with a friend.

I will not mention any of this to Greg Morrison when I enter
his office at the end of the day, of course. God knows what he
imagines his employees are thinking about as they scrape away at
the plaster. We are not machines. And yet indeed it may be that
I am the only one who gives a thought to the owners of the feet.
I wouldn't know, for I have been careful not to mention this to
the others.

It is not the sort of thing we talk about at lunch. Usually we
talk about the trouble Trevor is having with his pickup truck, the
trouble Ernie's having with his girlfriend's mother, and the
trouble Stella's having with her bank. We do not talk about me at
all. "How's things going with you, Monty?" someone will say, and
I'll say, "Okay, not bad I guess. All right." And that will be that.
Hal jumps in to complain about the size of cut the gallery takes
from the price of his sculptures. "I'll be working at this goddamn
place till I drop. What a country!"

Although he has little to say to me at lunch, Hal has lately
attempted the occasional conversation while we work. He is a
recent arrival, who has worked his way up to eleven feet a day,

though it is quite usual for one or two of them to come back to be done again.

"You say you paint murals?" he asked me one day.

"No."

"Oh. Sorry. I thought you said you were a painter."

"Why does everybody have to do something?" I said. "What's the matter with what we're doing right here?"

"Here? This is shit, man. We're just the chain gang." Hal thinks of himself as a sculptor. "We're just toiling away like little elves at our benches so's the fuckin' doctor can get rich."

This morning he asked me the name of the girl who sometimes came around to pick me up after work.

"Julie," I said.

"Girlfriend?"

"Sometimes," I said. "We lived in the same house for a bit – six of us."

"She gone?"

"Travelling."

Nothing more was said between us. Morrison came in at that point and stood watching for a while. Then he asked if I would step into his office at the end of the day. "Something we'd better discuss." He placed Earl Saxton of Fort St. John on the bench beside me.

⚘

I was wrong about what Morrison wanted. It is much worse. When he has closed the door behind me, he says, "I've got a letter here I want to talk about." He stands at the door a moment, as though he wants to make certain the rest of the employees are not able to hear. "From a doctor in Halifax." He runs a palm over

his slicked-back hair. I know what he is going to say. "Actually, I
didn't get the letter myself," he says. "Doctor Ford did. He asked
me to deal with it. No, actually, Monty, he told me to fire you. I
convinced him to wait until we see what you've got to say." He
lifts the letter off his desk a little, then settles it again. "This
fellow here, this podiatrist, he says he's got a patient who's been
getting mail."

Because I was still working at Stage One at the time, you might
say that in a sense I created her. That is, I received only her name
attached to a hollow cast. Donna Rossini. My task was to fill the
void with plaster and, when it had hardened, remove the husk –
giving her substance, and at the same time revealing her form. I
was not exactly new at the job, but I was new enough to have said
something like "Well, Miss Rossini, so we're about to spend a
little time together." It was the sort of thing you did, kidding
around, while you were not yet entirely used to the job. Also, this
was a remarkably graceful pair of feet, long and narrow and highly
arched, altogether suggestive of an attractive woman – long-
legged and poised.

In fact Miss Rossini and I were to spend more time together
than I'd anticipated. I was about to begin work on the next pair of
casts when Morrison came in and told me that he'd just sent
Carter packing. "I think you're ready to try Stage Two. Let's see
what you're made of."

So Donna Rossini and I moved on together. Hers became
the first feet I held in my hand for any length of time. In fact,
since I was having to learn the job from scratch she remained in

my hands for the rest of that day. We had plenty of time to get acquainted.

I held the left foot up to the window light. It seemed incredible to me that there was supposed to be something wrong with it. It looked perfect. A high arch. Lovely instep. Five perfect toes. A small round heel rising up to a slim ankle. No distortions, no lumps or bumps. I knew, even before I had taken up my instruments, that this was a woman in her twenties, someone light on her feet, graceful. I heard – so help me – the youthful sound of her laugh. Balancing the foot in my palm, I felt the warmth of her flesh. She had, for some reason or other, just placed her naked foot in my hand. And laughed. I knew the shape of her calf, of her thigh. She was lovely, lovely. I knew that she spent much of her time barefoot, and rocked her hips a little when she walked. When she was required to wear shoes she wore only the prettiest shoes she could find.

For a moment my partner stepped out of the room and I was alone with Donna Rossini. Quickly, I raised the foot to my lips, and kissed, one after the other, all of her toes. I did the same thing with the other foot. So powerful was the sudden sensation in my chest, in all my limbs, that I felt light-headed. Heat rushed to my face. I put the second foot on the counter beside the first, and stood trembling, with my eyes closed, while I tried to regain control. And yet, behind my eyelids, I saw precisely what Donna Rossini looked like, laughing down at me while I ran my hands up her calves. She had wide dark eyes and a pointed chin. Black curls framed her face against the blue of the sky.

"Daydreaming?" said my partner, returning. "You won't last long doing that."

Donna Rossini's was a simple problem to solve. She had a ten-dency to roll her weight onto the outer edges of her feet – no doubt when she was required to stand still, something she found boring. It was hard on her shoes. I worked the rest of the day to correct the fault, pleased that it was within my power to bring comfort to those moments of enforced boredom.

Examining my completed work, Morrison praised me for the promise I showed, then carried Miss Donna Rossini away to Stage Three, saying, "All you need now is to work twenty times as fast."

Morrison would think I was mad if I were to tell him the entire story. Instead, I tell him that it was only a whim. I meant nothing by it. Only a note in a bottle, so to speak. Hello from me. A child-ish prank, but certainly not meant to do any harm.

My heart is pounding so hard I am afraid it will shatter my ribs.

"Have you written to others? My God, have you been writing to them all?" He puts both hands on the top of his head and drops into his chair. Perhaps he is thinking of how many others there are in the storeroom.

I laugh. This has never occurred to me.

"Have you written to her more than once?"

"Five times, a half-dozen times, maybe."

"But Jesus, Monty, how the hell did you contact her in the first place?"

"That wasn't hard. One day at coffee break Corey asked me to cart a load of feet into the storage room. And while I was in there my eye fell on the name. I noticed that her doctor's address was in

Halifax. Then I wondered how surprised she would be to get a note from someone she'd never met." I do not tell him that I recognized the name, or that I remembered in detail how I had felt while working on her feet, and have felt ever since.

"You didn't write to her through the doctor's office, for chrissake – you idiot?" He shouts this. In fact, he is beginning to speak to me as he speaks to the others. Despite everything, I believe this to be a good sign. He is not treating me any longer as though I were fragile. He is speaking as though he would like to kick my ass.

"First I tried the telephone directory. Then I used other directories I found in the library."

It was a tedious but not unpleasant task to contact every Rossini in Halifax in my search for a Donna. When that did not turn her up, I began a search through the surrounding towns. Eventually, I located her in the town of Truro.

"I don't know, Monty. I just don't know what Ford is gonna say. The woman hasn't complained – that's the funny part. She just let it slip, apparently, while she was visiting her doctor. He says she thought it was funny. Maybe Ford'll overlook it this time, we'll have to see. But Jesus, Monty, you *moron!* What kind of thing did you *say?*"

∞

Dear Miss Rossini,

I don't mind that you accidentally informed your doctor about my letters. At least it didn't cause me to lose my job, though it was a close call and I have had to endure a number of jibes from my workmates ever since. Morrison says he didn't tell the others but somehow it got out. "Romeo," they call me. "Man of Mystery." They want to know if I'll be writing to Madonna next. They imagine that you show my letters around to your friends and have a good laugh.

I remember that in your second letter you showed some interest in Hal's sculpture, so you will be amused to learn that he has created a piece, in clay, which he has entitled "My Lady's Foot." I thought he intended to give it to me, as a joke, but in fact he has put a price of $700 on it, and has turned it over to a local gallery! When he brought it to work and left it for the day at the back of my bench, I waited until he'd gone to the washroom and then bent to kiss the toes, as I am sure he was waiting for me to do. It gives me pleasure to know that you understand.

You are quite right to suggest that I get back to filling my evenings at the drawing board, or the canvas. I have tried, though so far without success. I will continue to try. It is true, as you say, that I must not let a correspondence with a stranger become my entire life.

Aside from the teasing, little at work has changed. Morrison has gone back to speaking as though I were made of crystal. Perhaps I am. There are still too many feet coming back. He doesn't want to fire me, when it takes so long to train a replacement, but he has promised that if I do not soon increase my production again to twenty a day, with few returns, I shall follow in the footsteps of my predecessor, who is living on Employment Insurance and looking for work.

Julie has not written. I don't suppose she will. She believes I am too self-absorbed for any relationship to be a healthy one. She is a woman who tells you every thought, and then expects you to do the same. I, on the other hand, find it difficult to say "I wonder if you'd pass me the butter, please," if I so much as stop to think about it first. If I stop to think, I feel that it's hardly worth the trouble. I get up and get it myself, or do without. Or sit and feel exhausted at the turmoil that has been caused by the fact that the butter is beyond my reach. Often that is the loneliest time of all, when you are surrounded by people talking and can't bring yourself to break in to ask for something.

At any rate, I hope she is happy in Italy, where (I suppose, if the movies are correct) everyone will be hollering for the butter at the same time. Can you imagine how lonely a person would be in Italy if he once stopped to think, Does it really matter if I don't raise my voice to ask for what I want?

I would not have blamed you if you had not answered my first letter. Come to think of it, I would not be surprised if you had turned it over to your lawyer. A person cannot be too careful these days. I understand why you have written to say you have recently moved but wish me to use a post office box when I write. I am content that I will almost certainly never meet you, though it saddens me to think that I will never see for myself that

JACK HODGINS

you really have that way of tilting back your head when
you laugh, as I have imagined and as you have con-
firmed. Or that way of tilting down your chin to look up
from beneath your hair.

⌒⌒

Again and again I have tried to transfer this image from my head
to paper, and to canvas, but have not accomplished more than a
few unsatisfactory strokes. My hands refuse. Remembering the
secret warmth of imagined flesh, they will not transfer everything
they have learned to my waiting mind. Instead they continue,
day after day, to hold the deficient feet of strangers up to the
light, and to measure them with the precise instruments peculiar
to this service, and to form with damp white plaster the perfect
remedial shape that will – because of my knowledge, attention,
and skill – restore their balance.

THIS SUMMER'S HOUSE

Despite promises and careful planning, it was clear the family had missed the three o'clock sailing. This was hardly a reason, he knew, to feel so annoyed. The ferry traffic was always heavy on a holiday weekend; they may have arrived in time and yet been left behind for the next load. Or they may have stopped at a playground on the other side for the children to let off steam. No doubt they would be on the four.

Nathan Wagner felt much as he did before dinner guests arrived, though this uneasy tension made no sense today. He and Astrid were on holiday. The house was not their own. They were not expecting colleagues or new acquaintances but only members of their own family: their parents, their children, their grandchildren. Four carloads of them.

"Stop moving things, this isn't a stage set," Astrid said. "Take advantage of the extra hour of quiet. Walk down to the beach. Relax." The perfect hostess in her own home, she was lounge-chair horizontal on the deck of this rented house, in jeans and old T-shirt, reading a *People* magazine while dirty drinking glasses and lunch plates sat on the planking beside her.

He might as well wash them, since it seemed she didn't intend to do this herself. But for a moment he stood in the doorway looking at the strait beyond the low hedge of decapitated firs. A strong current was running the pale waves northward. A seiner slowly throbbed past, the voices of two men in red shirts barely discernible.

"If you need something to do," Astrid said, "empty the mouse-traps. Take them farther away this time. I swear the mice get back to the house before you do."

He scooped up the dishes from beside her. "I'm waiting until Spencer and Madeleine are here to watch."

If the mice died in their little tin box, he would be tempted to tell his grandchildren it was their parents' fault, for missing the ferry.

This was what it was all about. Not anxiety about being ready. Not irritation that they hadn't arrived when they'd said they would. It was because after a month of living in this summer's Gulf Island house, he was eager to show it off to the people he knew best, to admire its eccentric workmanship, to enjoy its absurdities, to encourage them to guess the type of people who owned the place, or the people who rented it for the winter months. His mother would not be in this year's house five minutes before guess-ing there was a potter's wheel on the premises. "Incense sticks crammed in this lopsided vase!" Of course she'd be right. Their daughter, Doreen, would rummage through the CDs and videos. "Headquarters for a terrorist group – learning how to bring loggers to their knees." She was able to say this nearly every year, in nearly every summer house, on nearly every island.

Nathan had nothing to do with finding or renting the house. This task was left to Astrid, who usually started her search in March. Last year's house was advertised in a friend's copy of the Teachers' Federation newsletter. The year before, she'd put an ad in local newspapers. This year she had asked Doreen to run her off a selection of rental houses from the Internet.

The house had to be on one of the Islands, had to be on waterfront property. It had to be quiet and comfortable enough for the two of them the whole summer, yet large enough for "the entire tribe," as Astrid put it, to sleep and eat in for one long weekend. A good water supply was essential.

There were to be no pets. Astrid's mother was allergic to cats – which meant, of course, that they jumped on her lap the minute she settled in a room. Last year's house, they'd discovered too late, was inhabited by two Persians – but these nervous creatures were confined to a single room with their own swinging door to the outside. Astrid's mother never saw them, hadn't guessed they existed, and hadn't said a word about her allergy.

It had become a yearly tradition. On the first weekend in August, Gerald would return from wherever his wanderings had taken him, and bring Astrid's mother across from Vancouver. Nathan's parents would drive down from Campbell River, Nathan and Astrid's daughter, Doreen, would come from Victoria, perhaps with a new man and perhaps not, and their son and daughter-in-law, Corbin and Sally, would drive from Nanoose, bringing the grandchildren Spencer and Madeleine. Enough people to stage their own performance of a Chekhov play, Nathan said, "If they weren't all too lazy to learn their lines."

Indeed some of the houses resembled stage sets, with several levels all opening like galleries onto a single room with soaring roof beams, angled staircases running up this side and that, and balconies for no reason at all in peculiar places. Last summer's house, a large farmhouse surrounded by sleeping verandas and fields of uncut hay, would have been perfect for *Uncle Vanya*. This year's almost demanded a Shakespeare. There were balconies and open spaces enough for *Romeo and Juliet*, a sort of indoor parapet for Hamlet's father's ghost. Every year Nathan suggested a performance for the following year, and every year they enthusiastically agreed to do it. Nathan's mother offered to make costumes because, as she said, "If I acted, I'd just upstage everyone and then you'd hate me." Astrid's mother, on the other hand, begged to play an ingenue "just once before senility makes an omelette out of my brain." On their last night together, they usually worked themselves up into a frenzy of helpless laughter, imagining next year's performance and all the things that could go wrong. But nothing ever came of it.

It wasn't because of laziness. There wasn't a lazy bone in the family. The children all led busy, energetic lives. Corbin and Sally between them held down three jobs. Doreen was a partner in a law firm. Gerald travelled with his band. They had the right to spend their holiday free of rehearsals. For them, just *imagining* their disastrous performances was enough.

"They come here to relax," Astrid protested, "as we do ourselves. They want to visit, not listen to a director shout instructions. I suppose you would be the director? Well, there you are. And where would we find an audience? Do you propose inviting the village to come and admire us? You can imagine what they would think."

There was always a village within walking distance of the house, though it was often only a general store and a gas pump, sometimes a café, with a few scattered homes nearby. When Nathan and Astrid entered the store or café, people watched them discreetly. Accustomed to summer visitors, they weren't curious enough to be rude. On the August long weekend, however, when Nathan and Astrid entered with their parents and adult children and daughter-in-law and grandchildren, people frowned openly. Suddenly it appeared that the couple had been the vanguard of an invasion. No doubt it was wondered how they could all fit under the roof of the Joneses' house or the Wilcoxes' bungalow. Did the Joneses know? Had the Wilcoxes given permission for this?

Of course they did, of course they had. Astrid always made sure the owners knew there would be a crowd for the one weekend. It was a matter of pride, to let others know that her family not only wanted to spend three days together but could survive the long weekend without doing damage to one another or to anyone's house. Invariably, the following week someone in the store would express astonishment that Astrid had looked so serene in the midst of all that company. "If a crowd like that dropped in on me I'd go screaming into the bush. Of course my family would tear each other to shreds before lunch. You must've done something right."

"Just fortunate," Astrid always said. Of course she was being modest. How many times had she challenged Nathan to come up with one thing that was more important than raising a family that cared for one another? It could not be left to luck. It required work. It had been, despite a part-time career as an accountant, her primary job.

For several years, village after village had been left with the memory of a tribe of lanky slope-shouldered long-necked tow-heads who had descended like a flock of snow geese and then flown off to somewhere else. If they remembered a name, it would be Astrid's. Astrid Something was the one who spoke to local strangers, dropped small hints about her life to those who served her, made a point of buying some local artisan's pottery. The potter would remember where this pot or vase or plate was to be displayed in Astrid's Victoria harbourfront condo. "Between my Walter Dexter bowl and the Matisse print."

No one ever asked Nathan what he did when he wasn't on their island. They assumed, he imagined, something professional, since he had a vague myopic look, a bookish appearance. Most of them wouldn't care, or wouldn't care to imagine that he had a life outside their field of vision. If they recalled him at all, it would be only as "The husband in Houston's place last summer – no, the summer before. Hair so pale you couldn't tell if it was blond or going white."

They would be surprised if he'd told them he painted people's houses, and even more surprised if he told them why. For thirty years he had been happy in a career as a freelance photographer, was successful at it too, with a reputation others envied. But then he had noticed that a day of doing what you loved went by in ten minutes while a day of doing what you disliked dragged on for ever. As a photographer, he would be an old man in a matter of days, furious that his life had gone by so fast. As a bored house painter, he could watch old age approach at a snail's pace while he had time to think, to daydream, to enjoy his grandchildren, admire his children, and slowly adjust to change.

Astrid considered this a perversion he would one day grow out of. She couldn't see the point in a long life if you spent most of it hating what you did. He knew she was right. On the other hand, this uncomfortable, dragged-out life as a house painter gave him the opportunity to get used to the passing of time. One day, far in the future, he might actually start to believe he could not live forever on this earth, and decide, "What the hell, I might as well

do what I like," as he had at the beginning. He hadn't sold his
equipment. He still had his eye.

The houses they rented were usually owned by Vancouver
teachers who'd decided to spend their summer travelling in
Europe or climbing mountains in Nepal, or by lawyers who'd
grown too busy to take advantage of their getaway homes. Often
these buildings were occupied by winter renters, who were turfed
out when Nathan and Astrid showed up, presumably to sponge
off friends or live in motels. Usually the dispossessed were
instructed to show the intruders the ropes, however irritating or
humiliating this must be for them. It was probably part of their
contract: cheaper rent if they saved the owner from having to
meet the summer folk. At first, Nathan had found this painful to
witness. Was it not bad enough to be kicked out of your home
without having to welcome the usurpers? But these people had
their way of taking revenge. "You'll find this bed sags in the
middle, you'll be fighting one another off all night. Of course the
water smells of sulphur. If you take too long in the shower you'll
drain the well and start sucking up blue clay. You'll be surprised
how bad it stinks when it gets that low."

Last summer's dispossessed was a painter who, before setting
out for a massage-therapy lodge in her Volkswagen van, made
them admire her most recent canvases, large oils of horses with
eyeballs rolled back in fear, or possibly fury. She seemed proud to
show them that the bathroom contained what she called an
earth closet, "since we try to be environmentally responsible
here." Yet she seemed eager to observe their faces when they saw
that what they were looking at was really an indoor privy. "This
isn't against the law?" Astrid had timidly wondered, anxious not
to appear disapproving of local customs. She believed all cultures

were equally valid, so long as they did not mutilate children or eat their elders. Although the artist insisted that the dial on the wall made some kind of magic take place in the shaft below, Nathan was convinced that it operated nothing but a fan some-where beneath your naked butt, a motor that hummed only so long as you stayed in the room – which was never any longer than you could help. For the long weekend of the family gathering, Astrid ordered a green plastic porta-john of the type used by con-struction crews, and had it set out at the farthest end of the prop-erty. "If they're going to have to put up with a privy they may as well have a healthy walk to get to it."

In fact, the outhouse had become a source of drama. Sally acci-dentally dropped a bracelet down the hole, and for two days kept increasing the value of the reward for anyone greedy enough to retrieve it. No one did, though ingenious methods were pro-posed. On the trail to the outhouse, Corbin staged a noisy mid-night fight with an imagined cougar, bringing all of them from their beds to find him smeared with ketchup and draped, half-naked, over the hood of his car. When he'd "come to," he dis-played scraps of big-cat fur in his hands. Sometimes Nathan suspected that his children came with props stowed in their vehi-cles, to help stir up as much excitement as possible.

"We use live mousetraps here," said this year's dispossessed renter, a young man in a flowered orange jumpsuit. He showed Nathan how to put cheese in the little tin boxes on the pantry floor, and then how to set the mice free in the orchard grass. Nathan was convinced he would be setting the same mice free every morning all summer. They would spread the word to all neighbourhood mice that a cheese banquet could be enjoyed with little risk, a few hours of not-uncomfortable confinement.

Nathan was tempted to leave the little buggers for two or three days before freeing them, to demonstrate that life was not the bowl of cherries the young man had trained them to expect. He hadn't done this, of course. And he knew he wasn't likely to find a killer mousetrap on this island. He would have as much success looking for DDT.

"And watch out for the wasp nest under the eave," the young man in the orange jumpsuit added as he was about to drive away. A tiny muscle jumped regularly at the outer corner of his dull left eye. The messy heap of camping equipment on the bed of his pickup suggested he was only moving across the island to camp in a park. Cooking on an open fire while Astrid and Nathan enjoyed the new electric range, shivering in a tent while Astrid and Nathan lolled about on a four-poster with a view of lights from passing yachts and distant mountain ski-lifts.

He'd dropped in a week later – the first renter to do this. His excuse was a forgotten kayak under the house. "Don't forget to use the fireplace," he said before leaving. "I built it myself." Perhaps he was warning them not to abuse the hand-picked beach stones he'd cemented into position with mustard-tinted mortar.

The next time he'd returned – a week or ten days later – it was for his toolbox. His old pickup had been acting up. He looked terrible, Nathan thought. Dark shadows under his eyes, hair uncombed, his flowered jumpsuit streaked with grease. It seemed that he was a bit of a handyman but had little to be a handyman *on*, aside from this house and his own dilapidated truck. "I ought to be doing something about that window," he said, nodding toward a swollen sash that wouldn't open. Before leaving, he'd made sure that Astrid knew he'd built the kitchen cabinets himself. She made noises of admiration, but later said, "Imagine being proud of doors that don't fit!" His carpentry was so awful, she said, and his appearance so pitiful, that she'd almost asked him for lunch. "Why didn't he disappear like the others?"

"Don't forget the wasp nest," the young man reminded them. Apparently he had noticed that nothing had yet been done about it.

Of course Nathan had got rid of the nest eventually. While there were just the two of them it was easy to put this off, but Astrid had only to say, "How would you feel if one of the grand-children?" and he knew the time had come to act. He walked to the store and learned, not too surprisingly, that the elderly gen-tleman eating triple-berry pie next door at the café counter owned the equipment needed for getting rid of wasps. Of course this gentleman claimed to have got rid of a nest in that same spot every summer for fourteen years. After promising to do the job for Nathan as soon as he'd finished his pie, he had needed only three telephone reminders before showing up at the house four days later.

Now the papery nest sat on the deck railing, waiting for the grandchildren. Madeleine might want to take it to kindergarten in the fall. Nathan moved it to a safer spot, down on the floor. Then he brought it inside and set it on the kitchen table, but decided to move it outside again to the railing. He felt as if an opening curtain had been delayed, leaving him with nothing to do but tinker with the set. What did you want the audience to notice first, when the curtain went up? What did you want them not to notice until later? These things made all the difference, in life as on the stage. You could breathe a sigh of relief only when it was finally too late to change your mind about anything!

The family made fun of him for it, of course, but the minute he'd deprived himself of his camera and begun to martyr himself on chilly scaffolds he started volunteering with a local theatre group. At first he was expected to take tickets at the door, and to sit in for truant prompters, but eventually it was discovered that his photographer's eye could be of use on the stage. "That set is a bit cluttery," he'd ventured to suggest, after much brooding about it. "And everything the same colour, the same size. Since this is a play about entrapment, you might want the audience's eye to go immediately to something suggestive – tall narrow windows, say, that look out on a concrete wall." After a period of awkward silence, he was invited to show them what he meant. Feelings had been hurt, unfortunately. The former stage designer discovered a conflict in his schedule. Nathan Wagner had more or less inherited the job.

Fortunately it was not a paying job, for he discovered that he loved it as much as he'd loved photography. If he'd done it full-time the days would start to fly again, and he would be aged and creaking in a matter of months. Even so, he could not avoid discovering similarities between the theatre stage and the painter's scaffolding. Though he resisted, his rebellious imagination pictured *Waiting for Godot* and *A Month in the Country* staged high up the wall of an apartment building, with an audience that stretched for several blocks. The hours began to fly by dangerously fast again, even on overcast days.

Of course he told no one about these fantasies. Perhaps this was why one of the highlights of this annual long weekend for him was the final evening when he proposed a performance for the following year and the family spent the rest of the evening

imagining the whole thing out loud, probable disasters and all –
especially the disasters, which could reduce a heartbreaker like
The Seagull to side-splitting farce.

"Imagine," Nathan once said in the midst of these hijinks,
"when Chekhov went off to his country house, the place was
filled not only with jabbering servants and all the arguing and
carrying on of his extended family, but also with neighbours, and
friends out from the city to stay for a week or so. Can you imagine
anyone writing a work of genius in the midst of all *your* racket?"

"Ah," Gerald said, "but did he try to get them to put on his
plays? Would they dare to make hash of his work like we do?" He
leapt to his feet and tore at his hair. "No respect, Olga! Surely, a
man of genius deserves some peace in his own *dacha*!"

"I'm disappointed that it is pronounced *datcha*," Doreen said.
"I would rather it was *daw-kaw*, which would seem more foreign
and substantial. Of course you had to be rich, so what difference
would it make to people like us how it was pronounced?"

Corbin said, "I wonder if the lower classes – house painters
without a country home of their own – rented a different *dacha*
every year."

"Idiot!" Doreen said, throwing a striped cushion against his
face. "The lower classes stayed home and starved! They were
lucky to have a *home*!"

"Which would," Nathan drew to their attention, "be owned by
someone else."

The family may have resisted staging his suggested dramas, but
they would arrive with board games to play in the evenings,
which could have much the same effect. The more frivolous the
game, the louder and more preposterous the competition. Losers
would prepare to commit suicide with their heads in the oven, or

climb to the roof while the others shouted extravagant encouragement, begging them to jump, or sometimes not. Poor losers told embarrassing lies about the winners, but would eventually be dragged into a chilling midnight swim. Winners would boast of their superiority in every second sentence until deposed by the following game, or threatened with having to watch the entire library of "eating healthfully" videos.

Astrid usually brought new ideas for games requiring more than just a table and a deck of cards. Last year she froze two blocks of ice in milk cartons and divided the family into two teams – male and female. The idea was to be the first team to melt its ice block without resorting to flame. Afterwards, much noisy discussion centred upon whether significance could be found in the fact that the women, after trying several other methods, had put their block in the electric oven, while the men (who'd won) had set theirs on the top of a running car engine. Doreen said she would go to the guillotine before admitting there was anything natural or inevitable about a relationship between women and stoves or men and cars.

"The guillotine?" Gerald said. "Then how about a firing squad? How do you feel about being garroted with a shoelace?" He started to undo one of his shoes in case she wished to prove her sincerity. "Would you give up your Grateful Dead collection?" No one was permitted to remain indignant or self-righteous for long, though Doreen complained that an internal-combustion engine depended upon a spark to ignite the fuel, and therefore the result was invalid anyway. They could not have a rematch, of course, since obviously both teams would dash for the electric oven.

"Do you think there's something wrong with us?" Nathan said. Astrid was no longer reading *People* but staring out across the water toward the snow-topped mountains of the bigger island.

"There's a good chance," she said. "How do you mean?"

"The other day at work Tom and I got talking about New Zealand again. I told him we'd considered emigrating, back when our kids were still home and could be dragged along, but we'll never do it now that we'd be leaving them behind. He thought I was crazy. Their grown-up kids have their own life, he said. 'If we moved to New Zealand they could visit once a year.' I didn't know what to say."

She got up from the lounge chair and came in to the house, kissing him on the chin as she squeezed past in the doorway. "Anita and Tom aren't us, Nate. Our bunch *want* to be together." She came back and put a hand on his arm. "They know you'll propose your silly performance and they will mock you so thoroughly that you'll have had your performance, though not the one you'd intended. I think I hear the ferry."

This house was close enough to the ferry slip that its thrumming engine could sometimes be heard when the breeze was right. If he went up on the roof with a pair of binoculars now he could probably see if any of them were on it. He wouldn't do this. He had done it once – he couldn't remember which island this was, sometimes they seemed to be all the one island in memory. When Astrid had told them, he disliked the faint shadow that flickered in some eyes before they'd begun to mock him. "Next year we'll find you piloting the ferry, just to make sure we get here." "If I'd known you were spying on us I would have mooned you from the car deck." Did they think he was getting too old to climb roofs, or were they insulted by his impatience?

"Now don't go looking at your watch every two minutes and sighing," Astrid said. "They could have missed this one too. It doesn't matter! It's a holiday! Even if they're on that ferry they could still stop for a while at the store."

This was shouted down from the bedroom. She came down the elaborate zig-zag staircase a moment later, wearing a pale green cotton sundress and matching sandals. She could wait until visitors were at the gate before deciding what to wear. Nathan dressed after his morning shower and seldom changed in the day. He did not, he supposed, think of himself as part of the set, to be dressed and redressed for any given effect. This bowl of sweetpeas, on the other hand, ought to be on the kitchen table where the sunlight would draw attention to them.

"My God, you're beautiful," he said, holding out a hand at the bottom of the steps. "Why didn't you put that on earlier, just for me? Now I'm not so sure I want them to come." He pulled her close and kissed her.

She responded warmly, but was sensible. He was more or less pushed aside so she could go to the kitchen sink and fill the kettle. "Your mother will expect tea."

The car at the gate wasn't one of theirs. It wasn't even a car, it was the rusty old pickup belonging to the young man of the flowered jumpsuit. He'd driven in through the gate and parked, and left his driver's door open while he came down the lane leaning a little to the left, rubbing one hand over his jaw and eyeballing this way and that as if looking for fault.

"Damn," Nathan said, and went to the door to meet him. "What did you forget this time?"

"I won't be a minute," he said. He looked past Nathan, perhaps hoping for Astrid, perhaps looking for damage to report. "I tore a hole in my tent and it rained in the night. The prediction's for more. I left my patching stuff behind."

JACK HODGINS

"Inside?"

He nodded. His eyes were red-rimmed and bunged up. Some of his unwashed ponytail had escaped from the elastic band. The flowery jumpsuit was well on its way to becoming a filthy rag. Unzipped nearly to the waist, it revealed a skinny chest as dirty as everything else. He might have spent his whole time under his truck, with every joint dripping steady oil and grease. Of course he stank of gasoline.

Nathan stood back to let him in. Have a good look around while you're at it, he thought. We haven't knocked your fireplace down. The cupboard doors are still overlapped and sagging. "I got rid of the wasps," he said.

"I heard," the young man said as he went past on his way to some other part of the house.

Astrid shot Nathan a look that warned against following. Freddie, he had told them his name was. Nathan could not recall hearing a surname.

This time the car in the yard was his parents' red Buick sedan. When his mother got out, she went back to push the gate closed. "Just leave it open for the others," Nathan shouted from the doorway. But his mother had already slid the bar across. "The others aren't behind us," she said as she came down the lane. "No sense letting in everyone's cows." She'd lived most of her life on a farm and believed that cattle dreamt incessantly of open gates to gardens they could eat and at the same time trample underfoot.

"There are no cows on this road," he said. "*What do you mean they're not behind you?*"

His father kissed Astrid and shook Nathan's hand. His mother hugged them both while she explained. "We met at that little mall as we'd planned, but the rest of them discovered a big sale on summer clothes. And then they ran into someone they knew from way back. They sent us ahead to tell you they'll be on the next one for sure!" To Astrid she said, "Your mother too."

"Can't resist a sale," Astrid said.

His mother tilted back and looked up at the house. "Ahhh!" Smiling, she held up her hands like a child expressing surprise and wonder. "A fairytale house! One, two, three, four, five gables at least! You must feel you're living in a magical place. When we came in the gate I sensed there might be a troll beneath the floorboards, but I don't think so now. A person could have a lovely honeymoon here!"

"A person?" Nathan's father said.

"Two persons!" She laughed.

"And it has a kettle!" she said. They could hear it squealing in the kitchen. "Certain rituals must be observed, and having tea before the weekend starts is one of them."

The tea had steeped by the time Nathan and his father had brought in the suitcase and the cartons of homemade bread and jam and pots of chili. As Astrid was about to pour, the young man stepped up from the pantry with a canvas satchel under one arm. Nathan assumed this was his "patching stuff."

Before he had time to say anything, Astrid put a restraining hand on his shoulder and introduced the young man to their guests. "Freddie lives here in the winter." She explained to Nathan's parents that Freddie had built the cabinets, had dragged those fireplace rocks up the cliff with a rope.

"Oh," Nathan's mother said. She had probably not seen mustard mortar before. "A fireplace can make all the difference. Especially near the water, where you must get chilly evenings."

Freddie hadn't taken his eye off Nathan. "You didn't empty the mousetraps," he said. It was a mixture of accusation and puzzlement. He might have been saying, "For some reason you have turned the pantry into a torture chamber."

Nathan laughed. Or tried to. "Only since yesterday," he said. There was little point in explaining that he'd been waiting for his grandchildren to arrive.

"If you like, I'll do it," Freddie said. That little muscle was jumping at the edge of his eye. You could see he would be on the phone to Vancouver within the hour. Nathan would be visited by the animal abuse people. Required to attend evening classes on the ethics of mice control.

"Well," Nathan said, fighting a wave of resentment. He addressed his parents. "Since you didn't think to bring the grandchildren, I'll have to do my parlour trick for *you*." He pushed past Freddie into the pantry and came out with the two shiny tin boxes, each the size and shape of a cigar box. "Listen," he said, and held one of them to his mother's ear. "Prisoners with uncut toenails." He turned it so that she could look in through the air slots. "How many?"

"My gosh!" she stepped back. "A crowd!" To Astrid she said, "Reminds me of the Marsdens' parties. Too many people, ceilings too low."

Nathan led the way up the lane almost as far as the gate, then veered into the uncut orchard grass where he set both tins down on a flat rock. "Ready?" He meant this for the young man too, who was standing just behind the rest of them as though to make sure Nathan went through with it. "Hear this, the rest of you!" Nathan formed a megaphone with his hands. "I'm releasing your relatives. Listen to their tale and you too can spend a night in a luxury hotel where nothing but the very best cheese is served for your dining pleasure."

"Nate," Astrid warned. Mocking local sensibilities was as bad as violating sacred customs. She would not go so far as to apologize to Freddie on his behalf, but she would find a way to express her regret. A thank-you card left on the kitchen table when they vacated. A note to the owners praising his concern for their comfort. *Freddie was considerate enough to check up on us, to make sure that all was going well.*

When the mice leapt free and immediately disappeared (five, six of them?), his father chuckled and shook his head as though he could never have imagined himself witnessing this. Nathan saw him wink at Freddie, as though to suggest the two of them were somehow separate from this nonsense.

His mother clapped her hands. "Where did they go, poor things?" It was impossible to know if they'd found holes in the dirt or had simply gone deeper into the grass. She turned her joyful smile on Freddie. Her bosom rose. "You see why we come? It's like running away to the circus once a year."

Their laughter flustered her. "You know what I mean. An adventure. Surprises and delights – but safe ones!" She squeezed Nathan's arm. "We'd be devastated if you stopped." Then she took hold of Astrid's elbow and the two of them started toward the house. She broke away, however, and turned back, when she saw that Freddie Millen wasn't following. "Where is he going?"

"Back to his campsite," Nathan said.

His mother appeared confused. This was not the way she thought things ought to be. "But we're about to have tea!"

Freddie, with his canvas satchel in one hand, was almost to the open door of his truck. "It's okay, ma'am," he called over his shoulder. "I got tea of my own."

"Of course you have," Astrid said. "But ours is almost ready." She, too, had turned back. He may not get an apology disguised as a thank-you card after all, he may get a cup of tea instead. Be a guest at his own table. Was she crazy? The rest of them, the whole houseful of them, would be landing in within the hour. Nathan had been waiting for *them* – their noisy greetings, hugs, suitcases dropped anywhere, food contributions shoved into the fridge, kids running through the house, everyone talking at the same time.

"He can tell us what it's like to live here in the winter," Nathan's mother said. She had started up the lane toward the young man, her hand out as though she would drag him back by the jumpsuit's zipper. She was a woman of immense curiosity, whose face always suggested she was prepared to like whatever she might learn. If she suspected he was the troll beneath the floorboards of this summer's house she was sure she could sympathize with his version of things. She'd never met a person she didn't want to love.

"I won't have no more winters here," he said. "Owners went and sold 'er." He gave Nathan a sidelong accusing glance as if he were somehow responsible for this.

"Oh, dear!" said Nathan's mother. She turned to him, expectant, as though this was something that ought to be dealt with immediately. Perhaps she, too, thought it was Nathan's fault.

"But where will you go?" Astrid said. "You can't stay at a campsite all year."

The young man shrugged as he backed away from them, inching closer to his truck.

"Now you *have* to come in for tea!" Astrid said.

"Otherwise," Nathan's mother said, "we'll feel we're turning you out of your own home." She's put a hand on Freddie's filthy arm.

Nathan watched the young man struggle with this. His good eye looked for those who might be tempted to sneer if he succumbed. Perhaps he wondered if he was too dirty to sit on the furniture. There would have to be newspapers under him.

Freddie was a shy boy now, probably a sick shy boy, but he could hardly be unaware of this old woman's knack for making you want to be part of whatever she was part of herself. She could end up asking him to build her a fireplace, if he returned to the house. It was Nathan he looked to, though, for something – help in escaping or permission to stay, Nathan couldn't tell which. Did he wonder if Nathan doubted his story of being permanently dispossessed? He did, of course. He did doubt it. But it probably didn't matter.

"You might as well give in," Nathan said. "When those two work together you haven't a chance."

When Doreen brought one of her lawyers, or Gerald his band members, it usually took Nathan a little time to adjust. He felt sorry about this, but there you were. He was slow to adjust to a good number of things. Astrid seemed not to make such distinctions. Once strangers came in the door, they were just part of the crowd. Of course his mother invited the singers and lawyers to bring their parents and siblings next time, and anyone else they cared about. If they were to take her up on it, each summer's house would have to be larger than the last.

They were all, even Freddie now, guests in this house – Nathan and Astrid's *dacha*, the young man's only home. Soon there would be the others – the ferry could be on its way again by now. If this fellow were here when the others arrived, the commotion would likely scare him off. And if it did not, Nathan Wagner, who'd had plenty of practice, would just have to find a way to help him fit in.

OVER HERE

"Will you take a look at this," my dad said. "This here is how you and me will make our fortune."

He opened a jackknife and ran a slit along the bark of a felled tree.

He'd chopped down three of them, chips flying. You had to hold up your arm to protect your eyes. The trees creaked and groaned as they tilted, then they fell with a swish. You could feel the thump through your feet. This was out in a back corner of the farm, where even the huckleberry bushes were tall.

Now he cut a ring around the trunk. Using his fingers and the blade of the knife, he started to pry off strips of bark. Thin as leather, orange behind the grey. The inside was wet and yellow.

"We'll set these out on the barn roof to dry in the sun," he said. "Then we'll sack 'em up and take them in to the depot."

The depot was where we took the beer bottles from Sunday-morning ditches, and burlap sacks of sticky fir cones in summer. They also paid for bark from the cascara trees.

"What will they do with it?" I said.

"Here, smell. You like that?"

He held the inside of a piece of bark to my face. A sharp sweet smell.

"Tastes good too," he said, "but I wouldn't go licking it, you'd spend the rest of the day on the run."

"What is it?"

"They make stuff in bottles out of it, for people who'd be glad to run to the toilet for a change. Here –"

He rooted around in his pocket and came up with another jackknife like his own, and gave it to me. Cracked mother-of-pearl on one side, with four different blades folded along the length. "You can do this just as good as I can. Start on that one over there."

I used both hands and leaned my weight into it. He gave me a flat wide chisel for where the bark didn't want to come away. The knife blade was wet. I didn't lick.

It was like skinning something alive.

It was like being one of the Indians we'd learned about in school. The Blackfoot, the Iroquois. Burning missionaries at the stake, cutting out hearts, peeling off a living man's skin. Putting on parties where they gave away everything they owned. Miss Percy cooked us all a pot of fish-head soup and then we sat under a tree and listened to her read from a book about a talking raven. You had to have courage to be an Indian. You had to be strong. Miss Percy had known an Indian who died in the recent War.

Any minute now a band of howling braves would burst into this clearing and capture me. They would scalp my dad and drag me off to be a slave in their village. I'd have to fight with the dogs for food scraps thrown to the ground. Until the day I saved the tribe from extinction. Then they'd reward me by making me their chief.

"You think there was ever an Indian village here?"

"Well now," my dad said. "Have you seen pictures of Indian villages in this part of the world?"

"Wooden longhouses," I said, "with totem poles out front."

"Always along a beach. Do we live on a beach, can you tell me?"

"The beach is two miles away."

"Well, do we live on a river filled with salmon then?"

"We don't even have a creek."

"What kind of Indians would build a village on this here gravel pit? They'd rather sit back and laugh at some idiot white man, breaking his neck to grow puny spuds and stunted hay from this goddamn rocky soil."

My dad drank from the wide-mouth Mason jar of cherry Freshie he'd kept in the shade. Then he leaned back against a standing tree and rolled a cigarette.

"Do you think there were any wars?" I said.

"Here on our ranch, you mean?"

It was never a farm, it was always a ranch, though we had only twelve acres left, most of it bush. One cow. Thirteen chickens. A pig.

"Tribes slaughtering one another," I said. "Battles."

"How would they ever find each other?" my dad said. "Back in them days trees here were as thick as the hair on your head. Didn't that teacher tell you anything? Wars happen on plains – the Plains of Abraham weren't thick with Douglas firs."

"We don't have any plains around here."

He set fire to the straggly tobacco at the end of his cigarette. "That's my point. They'd have their battles out on the water maybe, in their longboats. Or down along the beach."

"I guess I'll never find any arrow heads," I said.

"No Indian ever wanted this here place," said my dad. "They were smarter'n that. It took a bureaucrat in Ottawa to decide this land should be opened up. Gave it to Great War vets like your fool grandfather that didn't know nothing better than the rocks of Connemara."

Without their bark, the cascara trunks were as slick and pale as human flesh in the bath. The naked legs of giants.

There were no Indians at our school. Some Indians lived on a reserve twenty miles to the north, some lived ten miles to the south. They went to other schools. Miss Percy invited a woman from a reserve to speak about their way of life. She told us how they smoked salmon. She told us about making oolichan grease. Once, when a raiding party was coming south they sent their women and children to safety up into the mountains, but when they went to get them afterwards they'd disappeared. Nobody ever found them. Nobody even found bones, or footprints. Today, the band was mostly well-to-do fishermen with a chief who didn't look like an Indian at all. She held up a picture for us to see.

Then an Indian girl came to school, but she didn't know that that was what she was.

"And don't you ever tell her," said my dad.

"Why not?"

"The Tremblays would have your hide. You could ruin that little girl's life. They want her to have a chance to make something of herself."

A priest had driven up our road on Tuesday and handed her

over to the Tremblays, who lived across from us. On Wednesday she was sitting across the aisle from me in school.

"As if raising five boys of their own isn't enough work for that poor woman," my dad said.

The Tremblays were the only Catholics in this part of the district and had to drive all the way in to town for church. My dad was scared that Mr. Tremblay might take it into his head to donate a corner of his property for a church out here in the bush. Right across the road from us, he imagined. Right smack in front of our kitchen window. Cars boiling up dust down the gravel road, parking all over the place. Organ music ruining our breakfast.

"What did they tell her she was?" I said.

"Who knows? A child of God, maybe. She's got five brothers now to tell her she's the Queen of France."

Nettie Tremblay. I watched her out of the corner of my eye across the aisle. You weren't supposed to stare. How could you not know something that was known by everyone else? I could change everything, if I wanted. A scrap of paper with the information scribbled on it. No name. Just knowing I could do this made me feel warm and generous toward her. I was protecting her. We all were. One word and her life would be blown apart.

She'd go nuts and pull out her hair. She wouldn't be able to stand it. She'd kill herself.

Except, why wouldn't she want to know?

If we knew something about Nettie Tremblay that she didn't know herself, this could be true of me as well. When I turned twenty-one maybe I would find out that I'd been an Indian all along. Grandson of a Huron chief, sent out to learn the ways of the white man before being called home to rule my people. I wouldn't fall apart when I heard. I'd have my own hut, my own animal skin robes. I would have my own slaves who did everything I told them to do. I'd be the richest man in the tribe.

⤠⤝

On Saturdays my father cut down half a dozen trees and left me to peel cascara bark on my own. He'd gone off on some new plan for getting rich. Nettie Tremblay came across to watch. I offered her a share of my allowance if she'd fill the gunny sacks and help me lay out the bark on the roof of the barn.

"You like the smell of that?" I said.

She nodded. It was a pleasant smell. Sometimes it was almost impossible not to lick the inside of the bark, except that you remembered what would happen.

"I guess you've eaten bark before," I said.

"No," she said. "Why would I?"

"Which do you like better," I said, "smoked fish or beef?"

"I don't know."

Her eyes went blank, as though she'd gone away inside. She must have been lying.

"Do you like to eat berries?" I said.

"Sure," she said. She snatched huckleberries off a nearby bush and ate them.

"Not like that," I said. "You break off a whole branch, like this. Then you carry it around."

"There was a war here once," I told her. "Right where we're standing. An Indian war. Seventy-six braves were slaughtered right here, their blood soaked into the earth. Some of them were skinned alive. Had you heard about that? You could be standing right on top of a Kwakiutl skull."

She wasn't interested in my war. She carried slabs of bark to the gunny sack and stuffed them inside.

"I wouldn't mind being an Indian," I said. "*Hyas klahowyum nikt.*"

I'd memorized some Chinook, since I didn't know which language I would need when the time came.

Maybe she wasn't impressed. She made a face. "I'm going to be a movie actress."

"You can't be a movie actress."

"Why not?"

"Because you can't."

"I can if I want. Why can't I?"

"Because. You don't look like a movie actress."

"I will when I'm older."

"No you won't. They'll make you go and be a servant to the nuns."

She blew a raspberry. "Maybe I'll be a nun myself."

"I bet you won't. I bet you'll have eighteen kids and some of them will die."

She dropped her armload of bark to the ground and started to leave.

"They won't die," I said. "I'll be a doctor by then and I'll save them."

Nettie Tremblay's skin was the dark red-brown of the soil around rotted stumps. Her hair was black as crows, but it was not parted down the middle with two long braids at the back. Mrs. Tremblay hacked it off short and curled it. She didn't have the beauty of a Mohawk girl in a book. She was chubby. Her face was wide and quite flat, like the drunks outside the Lorne Hotel.

"Are there any Indians in our family?" I asked my dad at the supper table. He was prying stubborn eggs off the frying pan.

"Not so nobody'd notice," he said. "Some figured Aunt Elsie's Frank for one, but he turned out to be just another Italian."

He put my plate down in front of me. Fried potatoes with an egg broken over them. Boiled peas.

"I mean in our veins," I said. "Uncle Leo's pretty dark."

Uncle Leo was my mother's brother. Maybe my mother had had Indian blood in her veins. Maybe when she went off for a better life she'd gone to rejoin her tribe.

He pulled in his chair and started forking up his food. My dad ate fast, hardly noticing what he was doing. His left hand picked at the flaking paint on the table.

"I'd like to be an Iroquois," I said. "No, I'd like to be a Blackfoot and live in a teepee. Moving around. It'd be fun to shoot buffalo."

"I'd rather be a Haida myself," my dad said. "Then I could lie around carving sticks of wood while my slaves did all the work."

He could say things that made you wonder if he read your mind. He winked. The patch of bared table grew larger every day, like a continent expanding and changing shape, eating up the paint.

"Maybe you'd rather be one of their whalers," I said. "In a boat hollowed out of a log. Throwing spears."

"I wouldn't like that at all. I'd have to drag the whales back to shore and cut them up. Too much work." He mopped the broken egg yolk off his plate with a piece of bread. "Then I'd have to eat the blubber," he said. "I guess I'll stay the way I am, ignorant and poor and white. At least I've got spuds on the table, and once in a while a chicken."

Maybe even beautiful Iroquois maidens had flat plain faces when they were young. Maybe Nettie Tremblay would be pretty when she grew up. She'd never be a movie actress, but she might be beautiful enough to marry.

Our children would be half-breeds. Half Indian, half mongrel Irish. We'd go in search of her roots, and find out that she was a hereditary princess. The first thing I would do is order a raiding party to go off and capture a dozen slaves – white, brown, it didn't matter. My father would be amongst them. Maybe I'd pretend I'd never seen him before. My throat tightened when I thought of this. My father would give his life for me in a minute, but I was an ungrateful son who would take my time about deciding what to do with him. After all, he'd had no business kidnapping me and bringing me up as his own.

∽

The brothers kept an eye on her at school. Five wild Tremblays – Lucien, Paul, René, Pierre, Antoine. They'd kill you if you told.

They'd kill you even if you said something to someone else. You could never find out who else had been warned. Everyone, you guessed. Because anybody could see what she was. Anyone could blurt it out.

You couldn't take a chance. Even if you said, "Look at the squaw scratching her bum," it could be to someone who might tell her and you'd be to blame. Nettie Tremblay would go nuts. And the brothers would rip off your head.

You'd never get off the school bus alive. And if you did, you'd never run fast enough to get home. And if you did, they'd climb in through your bedroom window and smother you with your pillow. After they'd pulled all your teeth, and cut off your dick.

Paul Tremblay was sixteen, still in Grade Five, a hundred and seventy pounds. He could do that all himself, while the others sawed off your toes.

If you whispered for Nettie to lend an eraser, you could see Pierre trying to hear what you said.

If you looked too long at Nettie, you'd find Miss Percy glaring. She wasn't as scary as the Tremblay brothers, but she folded her arms like a sentry on guard, her face clenched up like a fist. Paul Tremblay asked her to a movie once, but she laughed. So he rammed his elbow into Warner Hilton's nose. It was a bloodbath. Miss Percy mopped it up.

There were no more lessons about life in an Indian village. No more stories about ravens. We learned about Incas and Mayans instead. They threw maidens into wells but never set foot on this island.

You couldn't even be mean, not without risking your life. When Neil Saunders made a face behind Nettie's back, the brothers dragged him into the woods and beat him up. Then they took off his clothes and left him behind a tree. They stuffed his pants and shirt down the toilet but passed his underpants around on a stick.

Nettie Tremblay didn't notice. She did her work. She ate her lunch. She smiled and nodded if you said a few words, but she acted like someone who lived in a world with glass around it.

You'd think being so protected would make her proud. But she didn't stand with her gaze on the horizon, like an Iroquois princess waiting for the warriors to come home. She walked with her head tilted down, her eyes on the ground. She scuffed along with one pigeon-toed foot in front of the other. She wasn't like an Indian at all, not the Indians we'd read about in books. Not

the Indians Miss Percy had told us about in her lessons on Our
Proud Neighbours.

Nettie Tremblay didn't know how much trouble we went to, to
keep her ignorant, or she might have tried a little harder. After a
while you wondered if she was worth it.

She was different on Saturdays, though. She talked a blue
streak while she helped me with the cascara bark. She didn't
want to be a movie star any more, she wanted to be a nurse. She'd
be a nurse for a while and then a doctor, in a giant city hospital.

Her brothers didn't follow when she came across the road. It
was because they trusted me, my dad said. The Tremblays knew
what sort of people we were, over here.

⌘

One day she showed up at the bus shelter wearing glasses. Purple
frames. Who ever heard of an Indian wearing glasses?

"Why are you wearing those things?"

"So I can see better," she said.

"You could see before."

"Doctor says I'm short-sighted, like Miss Percy."

She pushed them up with her thumb. She didn't have enough
nose to keep them from sliding down.

Four eyes, they called her when we got to school, but not
where her brothers could hear.

Goggle face.

Everyone wearing glasses was called something. It didn't count.

The next day she showed up at the bus shelter wearing lipstick
as well as the glasses. No girl in our class wore lipstick, you had to
be thirteen or fourteen for that. It didn't make her look pretty, it
made her look dumb.

"Does your mother know you painted your face?" I said.

"My mother's the one put it on."

She opened her lunch bag and showed me a lipstick tube next to her sandwiches. Maybe her mother wanted to make her feel better about wearing glasses.

"Warpaint," I said.

"It makes you look cheap," Alice Laitinen said. The Tremblay brothers weren't close enough to hear. They'd murder Alice if they'd heard her, even if she was a girl.

"You better wipe it off before we get to school," I said. "You don't want to look like a tramp."

Tramp was my dad's word for women who painted themselves up and smoked and swung their purses. My mother had not been a tramp, but she'd thought she was too good for us.

It didn't really make her look like a tramp. Tramps were supposed to be pretty, even if they looked cheap. She probably thought the lipstick made her look pretty, but it didn't. She needed someone smarter than those brothers to protect her. She would make a fool of herself.

I sat beside her on the bus. Her brothers sat at the back, but you could be sure they kept an eye open. You had to be careful they didn't hear. Lucien. Paul. René. Antoine. Pierre.

"It doesn't suit you," I said. "It doesn't look nice on you the way it does on some girls."

She looked out the window.

"You're not old enough," I said.

She pulled in both her lips as though she might swallow them. This flattened her nose. She had to push her glasses up again.

"You don't want people to laugh at you," I said. "You're not like Shelley Price."

Shelley Price was fourteen, six grades ahead of us. She was blonde, and pretty. She was the first girl to wear nylon stockings to school.

"Drop dead," she said. "I'll do what I want. Go sit somewhere else."

I hated her. She didn't even know how lucky she was. I didn't *have* to feel sorry for her.

"West Coast Indians aren't real Indians," I told my dad that night. "Charlie Morris said they came from China on a raft."

"That must've been some raft," my dad said. "I'd like to see it."

"I'd rather be an Algonquin," I said.

"Good idea," my dad said. "You'll be closer to Ottawa. You can dance for the Great White Father when he's in town. Tell him he's welcome to a night on the kitchen cot if he's ever short of funds in this neck of the woods."

⁓⊝⁓

The whole south slope of the barn roof was covered with bark. The slabs were nearly dry enough. Some had curled up, and cracked when I stomped on them. Their colour was a dark red now. I thought of the little bottles, for people who couldn't go to the toilet without some help.

From the peak of the barn I could look out over the small green field. The pig's smelly pen was below. Our house had not been painted since some time before I was born. Flecks of white were stuck here and there on the weather-blackened boards. My dad was going to paint it one day soon.

When Nettie came across the field I said I didn't need her today.

"You can go home. My dad didn't cut any more trees."

She came up the ladder anyway.

"You want me to go so you won't have to pay me," she said.

Maybe that's why she'd kept coming over. Money. She wouldn't talk to me at school any more, but she talked to me while we worked.

She came up the roof on all fours, and sat on the peak beside me. She didn't wear lipstick on weekends, but she wore her glasses every day.

"How rich will we be?" she said.

"I don't know. My dad never said how much they pay."

"How do you know you'll get any of it?"

"He gives me an allowance."

"Most of it's gonna be mine."

"Not most."

"You said fifty cents for every day I helped."

"I didn't say that."

"You did so."

"You didn't help all day, you only helped for a couple of hours each time. When you got bored you went home."

"He won't pay you anyway," she said. "You won't get any allowance, he needs the money for groceries. My dad, he says you're only a step away from the poorhouse over here."

I felt myself go stiff all over. "Whaddaya mean?"

"Just look at this place," she said. "My dad, he says a man with one arm and a wooden leg could make better use of it than your father does."

"You're lying," I said. "My dad's always been nice to Mr. Tremblay."

"He says if you were Catholics the priests would take you away from your father and put you in a home."

"That's dumb," I said. "Nobody's going to take me away."

"You don't know everything. Maybe somebody will. Somebody could be coming to get you right now. You don't know everything."

"Oh yeah?" I slid a little farther away from her on the roof peak. "I know something."

"What?"

"I know something you don't know."

"What is it then?"

"Something about yourself."

"I don't believe you."

"If I tell you, you have to promise you won't tell anyone else. You have to promise you won't tell anyone that I told you."

It was like standing on the edge of a cliff. She was at my mercy. She had always been at my mercy. One word and over she'd go. Nothing would be the same.

"I won't believe you anyhow. You lie."

"I won't tell you then."

"Tell me."

"Promise?"

"Okay, I promise. What is it?"

"What do you think you are?"

"Whaddaya mean?"

"What kind of ancestors do you think you have? Do you think you're a Swede?"

She laughed. "Don't be stupid."

"The priest brought you here from somewhere. Don't you remember?"

She went away from behind her eyes again. She didn't deserve to know. I wouldn't tell her. She could be a Haida princess. She could be descended from Big Bear. She could be Sitting Bull's niece. But she didn't deserve to know. Let her think she was just an ordinary girl who looked stupid in glasses and lipstick.

"What do you think you know?" she said.

"Nothing."

"You better tell me, you think you're so smart."

She stood up and hit me across the head with a slab of bark. "Stupid! Stupid! Stupid! Stupid!"

She hit me again and again. Then she scrambled down the roof and turned to go down the ladder. "Stupid stupid stupid."

⁕

"She knows, doesn't she?" I said to my dad. "I bet she's known all along."

"I suppose she must've," he said.

We were filling the burlap bags, for the trip to the depot in town. Nine sacks. First we'd broken the dried bark into smaller pieces.

"And you knew she did too," I said.

"I suppose I did."

"So why'd you tell me not to tell her?"

"Everybody was told not to tell her. Do you think if they'd just asked everybody not to call her names they wouldn't? Did you hear anyone call her names?"

"No."

"And why is that, do you think?"

"Because of the brothers."

"The brothers aren't always there. The brothers wouldn't be in the girls' washroom, for instance. Do you think anyone ever called her things in the washroom?"

"I guess not."

"I guess not," he said. "Do you know why people would've called her names, if they had?"

"I don't know," I said. "To make her cry? To make themselves feel better'n her?"

"I'll tell you why they didn't. Because they were part of a conspiracy. They didn't have to call her names, they could feel superior just by being part of a plot to keep her from knowing the facts. Them Tremblays are not so dumb."

The gunny sacks leaned against one another with their tops gaping open. My dad began to tie them closed with binder twine.

"Was anything said between you?" he said.

"Not much."

"Then leave it up to her. Maybe she'll go to school in beaded moccasins one day and tell you to call her Laughing Squirrel."

I thought about this while I watched him stitch up the gunny sack. "It isn't fair."

"Maybe she'd agree with you there," he said.

"What would they do if I wore animal skins to school and told them to call me Mighty Warrior?"

"They'd laugh in your face."

"What would they say?"

"Worse than they'd ever say to Nettie Tremblay, I'll tell you that. Maybe they'd just tell you to your face what they say behind your back."

This was something new. My skin felt funny and cold.

"What do you mean? What do they say behind my back?"

"Maybe there's more than just one plot out there, I bet you never thought of that. Do you think there isn't something they could say about us, if they decided they didn't give a hoot for your feelings?"

He winked. We're not so dumb either, is what he meant. We know who we are.

"I don't know," I said.

"You don't? Then they must have a better grip on their tongues than I thought."

"Anyway," I said, "it wouldn't be my fault."

He laughed. "Poor baby, stuck with me for your old man. Let's get these buggers onto the truck and outta here."

I could have killed him then. It wasn't fair. I was the one who should have been related to Big Bear. I was the one who ought to be Sitting Bull's son. You can be sure I'd stand up and give them a fight. I'd chase the white people right off the land, I'd drive them into the sea. I'd make them all go back to Ireland where they'd have nothing to eat but rotten spuds and rocks and rain, where you could die from just being poor.

DAMAGE DONE BY THE STORM

By morning, everything has been thrown into doubt. More than a metre of snow has fallen during the night, and even the most efficient removal crew in North America has not been able to handle it. According to the radio, a family car has gone off the road in the Gatineaus, somersaulting off a bank to explode in fire. Anyone who tries to drive in this is crazy.

Alfred Buckle is in a state. Just recently retired from the Senate, he is impatient with everything, especially with anything that cannot be brought to a vote. Today, it's the weather. When his wife appears for breakfast, he has nothing prepared but toast. He has been on the telephone. The storm has missed their grandson's village; the Grand Opening will go ahead as planned. Buses cannot be trusted but trains are running, though not necessarily on time. "He'll have to treat us like heroes when we get there, risking our lives when we could have stayed home by the fire."

"Oh dear." Judith Buckle twists her rings. Her eyes seek inspiration from the nearest wall of paintings. Snow scenes. Nudes. Overlapping smears of indeterminate colour. Bits of feather glued to peaks and ridges of solidified oil. "I shan't go," she says, and places both hands on the lace-edged tablecloth. "Warren wouldn't want his ol' Gran to break her neck."

"While a grandfather's neck," suggests the Senator, "is of no real consequence."

"You've made a lifestyle out of risking yours." She pours coffee for them both from a silver pot. "I can't imagine you changing now."

The Senator makes a throaty sound to suggest his modest agreement. "The real risk, for me, would be in *not* going – as you know. I don't see that I have any choice."

This morning Judith Buckle is a dainty woman in a blue dress, with pale amber hair. On a blue-and-amber morning her face and hands are covered with the copper speckles of a former redhead. At seventy-six she is steady on two-inch heels.

She has several versions of herself to present to the world. She was a teacher long ago, and still occasionally does a bit of tutoring. She was a mother too, of course. After their daughter died, the Buckles raised their grandchildren here in this house – their father having remained in the west. Throughout much of her husband's time in the House of Commons and later the Senate she was a popular Ottawa hostess, known for her dinner parties. Now that he has retired to private life, she volunteers at the National Gallery, and sometimes conducts tours in this house beside the canal. New acquaintances are often curious about her collection, most of which have been donated by artists grateful for a day or two of free board.

That the house is seldom without overnight guests is entirely Judith Buckle's doing. She has a weakness for artists and "folks from home" in need of a bed. At any moment one or two of their bedrooms may be occupied by West Coasters passing through. Students, assistant-professors doing research, couples travelling on a shoe-string, families discovering expenses far worse than they'd expected before leaving home – so long as they are from west of Hope and in serious need they are welcome. At the moment, honeymooners from Sechelt are still breathing away at the end of the upstairs hall, late risers every day this week.

The Senator has little to say about this, except that he will make toast, nothing more. The coffee is Judith's department. If anything more than toast and coffee is wanted, they can make it themselves. And if they are to sleep under his roof he expects them to listen while he offers his thoughts on the elected lunatics who seem determined to destroy their home province, and his.

Today he will not be here to greet the honeymooners when they come down, or to lecture them on the follies of British Columbia politics. He has a train to catch. He has a short speech he is anxious to give. Judith will fry bacon and eggs for them, he suspects, once he has gone. She will start pancakes the moment he's out the door.

"Now don't move," she says, "while I get us some of that –"

She leaves the room in the middle of sentences, a habit she acquired as a politician's careful wife. In this way, she never has to finish a thought and face the consequences. When she returns with a jar of Smucker's marmalade, she asks him to do something about the light bulb in her kitchen. "All that flickering makes me think I'm in a Charlie Chaplin film!"

"When I've returned," the Senator says. "If I'm to break my inconsequential neck doing *favours*, I'll wait till after I've been to congratulate the boy. And have drunk my share of his wine."

"Which reminds me," she says. "I must send the tin of butter tarts I made for the occasion. Don't let me forget."

As he sets out for the train, laying down the imprint of his boots on the crisp white surface, he passes other men standing on doorsteps with their shovels, uncertain where to start. "Hit and run!" he calls, indicating the sky, which is a clear innocent blue. Guilty clouds have scurried into hiding.

He keeps to streets untouched by civic crews, though the air is noisy with the sound of graders pushing snow off the major streets and the *beep beep beep* of trucks backing up for loads to haul away. Toward the end of a block he greets a young couple digging into a snowdrift to see if their car is inside, then quickens his pace for the train. In the crook of one arm he carries the tin of butter tarts, which Judith has not forgotten to give him. Judith Buckle is known for not forgetting.

She is known, especially, for not forgetting how it felt to be a newcomer to this city. Judith Buckle long ago set herself up as Ottawa hostess for West Coasters new to exile, as she once was herself. It is foreign territory here, she would say. The first thing you'd better get clear is that these people don't imagine what you've left behind. It's so far away it might as well be Tibet. In fact, they would prefer that you'd come from Tibet, which would make you interesting. For several years her March Break-up parties were famous amongst those who could hardly believe a winter could last so long. She gives smaller versions, now that he has retired, while the ice creaks and snaps and piles up along the river. This year's invitations are stacked on the dining-room table, awaiting addresses and stamps. Later, when the honey-mooners have been fed and entertained at length with her tales of a life as a political wife, and with instructions on what to see and what to do in the city, she will shut the door behind them and settle to begin the task of addressing the envelopes.

Later, he knows, she will make telephone calls to fellow members of her arts-funding Foundation. If the streets have been cleared by afternoon, and if the buses are running, she will head west on Carling to visit an old friend, Betty Borleski, in hospital. On the other hand, if the streets do not improve, she will keep herself busy at home with a few more chapters of her book-club book, a few more squares on her charity quilt, and an agenda planned for the next meeting of the Foundation.

"One snowfall too many," says the woman who sits facing him near the rear of the third coach. She sits with her ankles crossed and wears one of those quilted coats that look as though they are meant for walking through fire. "You'd think a disaster'd hit the city, the way people react." She glances at Senator Buckle, then at the youth who sits beside her with a leg out in the aisle. "You expect to see heaps of rubble, with buildings collapsed."

"A bus in a tree?" the Senator suggests.

"Or some farmer's cow on the roof of the Parliament Buildings." She peers out the window as though she might actually see what she has just invented. Her boots, trimmed with fur and united at the ankles, swing up nearly level with the Senator's knees, and then down again to the floor.

Up near the front of the coach, youngsters in woollen tuques hoist skis onto the luggage racks and try to find seats together. A woman in a maroon coat with snow on her shoulders works her way down the aisle and pauses to glare at the Senator before taking a seat with her back to him. The elderly man beside her wears a glossy wig that overhangs, like thatch, a hairless neck.

"It must be important," the quilted woman says, "to be travelling on a day like this. I have a funeral I mustn't miss."

The Senator places his gloves and fur hat on the seat between him and the tin of butter tarts. A slab of nearly transparent snow drops from the toe of his boot. "My grandson," he says. "He's opening a business today and I promised to be there." He places a hand against his coat pocket to hear the sound of paper. "And to deliver a speech."

A short speech, of course, but it is his first since retiring. He was well known for his speeches in the House, and later the Chamber – for his wisdom, for his sober second thoughts, and for the pleasant sonority of his voice.

The woman seems pleased with what she has heard. "A grand opening!" But her smile quickly turns to a frown. "Will he go ahead with it now, in *this*?"

"He claims the locals will come."

The young man looks up from his magazine, perhaps wondering what is so special about this grandson that neighbours can be counted on. His broad face is pale, his hair the colour of rust.

The Senator does not offer more. It is no one else's business that Warren and his lady friend have converted an old flour mill. Or that his grandson is opening a shop for local arts and crafts.

The young man returns to his magazine. A boy, really. On the seat between him and the woman there is a newspaper whose front page is dominated by large red headlines, shouting about the snowfall they can see for themselves out every window.

The woman glances at a tiny watch on her wrist. "Let's go," she says. And, as if the engineer has been waiting for her permission, they begin to move out from the station, slowly, wheels grinding beneath them, a bell clanging somewhere behind. Down between two high white banks of snow. The sound of the wheels turning. The sight of rooftops sliding past.

At least they are moving. The Senator, having given himself up to dependable forces, feels tension draining from somewhere inside. *Ladies and gentlemen: it is impossible to express what a pleasure it is for me to be here today. For I can remember –*

"A stranded bus," the woman says, looking out the window. Again her locked-together boots swing up, and then down to describe a quick arc in the muddied snowmelt on the floor.

The Senator contemplates asking the boy for the newspaper, but decides against it. A storm like this one tends to make news of the world irrelevant. And as for reports from the Hill, in retirement he has trained himself to avoid political news in public, since it tends to have him raving at strangers.

"A horse stiff as a statue in that yard," the woman says. "I wonder what he thinks of us."

"He is a horse," the Senator says. "He is aware of his growling stomach, nothing more."

Soon they have left the city behind, and its suburbs, and are passing through an area of white fields and blanketed farm buildings, the silos wearing soft white caps.

"An abandoned car," says the woman facing him. The abandoned car sits under a roof of snow as deep as itself. Soon there is another, and a third – the white lumpy shapes of cars deserted along what must be the buried road. Possibly this is the road that he and Warren took when they drove out in this direction the one time the boy took him fishing, though it is not easy to believe he is looking at the same expanse of fields and woods that were so green and leafy then.

The boy was still living at home at the time. With the canoe on the roof of Warren's rusty Corolla, they'd driven out of town on the Queensway, then down a narrow highway and up a dusty concession road. They twisted through low hill country, past faded farmhouses and sagging fences grown over with honeysuckle and weeds. A farmer came out of his barn with a bucket in each hand and stopped to watch them pass, his face as empty and uncomprehending as the face of his cow. Below a small dam, they put the canoe in a river and paddled downstream through woods and fished in his grandson's favourite spot for the whole warm day.

The Senator had little real interest in fishing but kept this to himself. They had done far too little together, he and the boy. He caught twenty or thirty bass, but threw them back. Not one was long enough to keep. Tails were attached to heads directly behind the gills. Warren caught a large pickerel, but threw it back as well. "At his age he'll be full of poison."

Late afternoon on the river they'd come upon a broad-chested, middle-aged fellow sitting on the bank. "Percy," the boy said. "He farms above." They pulled up the bottle of rocks they'd been using for an anchor and paddled to shore. This Percy sat on an old car seat – just rusty springs and shreds of tattered fabric. According to Warren, he sat there afternoons when the weather was good, just watching the water flow by. It seemed he knew the boy. He screwed the lid onto a jar of clear liquid, tucked it under the rusted springs, and invited them up to the house.

The farmer's daughter came out of the kitchen to shake the Senator's hand and went back to bring out homemade cider and scones. She was a little shy, soft-spoken, attractive in a way the Senator considered pleasantly old-fashioned. You couldn't imagine her in anything but that loose cotton skirt, with her hair in a single long braid. She nodded solemnly at this nineteen-year-old boy as though he were just another of the countless city fishermen her old man dragged up the hill from the river to sit in her living room listening to talk about the declining profits in beef. There were a few white-faced Herefords in his field. The farmer was beginning to think a fellow might as well let them graze until they died of old age for all the money people were willing to pay for the meat. The young woman smiled and crossed one leg over the other to admire her own slim ankle, and paid little attention to the visitors.

It was nearly five o'clock before they started paddling the three or four kilometres upstream to the car. At a narrow part of the river, something different began to happen to the water. As if it had swollen, or been put on a stove – like the surface of boiling jam. It swirled and rolled back on itself, formed dimples and whirlpools and patches as wrinkled as crepe. Paddling had got more strenuous. Did the boy know what he was doing? The Senator's shoulder began to ache. He noticed a large tilted birch to his left that didn't seem to move. They were paddling as hard as they could only to stay where they were. "I can't keep this up," the boy behind him said. "It's the dam. I can't paddle any harder than this." In the split second of their pause, the canoe was whipped out into the centre of the river, turned backwards, turned again, and they went hurtling down this mad rush of current. This was the way it would end, the Senator thought. His grandson had brought him out to where they would both be drowned. Which of them could save the other? "I'm steering for that little bay!" Warren yelled. They hurtled across the current to a point of land, then shot into the calm backwater behind it. The boy threw the anchor up on the bank and clambered onto the land, then wrapped the rope around a stump.

Attempting to follow, the Senator slipped and got wet to his hips. It was necessary for the boy to grab him under his armpits and haul him up out of the water.

Even after he'd secured a foothold in the grassy bank, he kept a hand on Warren's shoulder. They laughed, and hollered foolish curses at the treacherous river. Boy and old man, happy to be alive.

"Do you think any jury'd believe you didn't bring me out here to drown me?" the Senator said. "You would have to drown your grandmother too, and do it before she'd spent your whole inheritance on questionable pieces of art."

Warren apologized for forgetting that extra water was released through the dam every day at the same time. The Senator was tempted to lecture, turning this into a lesson in being prepared, doing your research – but decided against it. The excitement of the close call and the exhilaration of the rescue had become a satisfying climax to the day. He didn't want to spoil that. He didn't want to say anything that would spoil his chances for similar excursions in the future.

"A steeple," says the woman facing him. "There's a little town over there." She hums after her own sentences, as though agreeing with herself. The young man beside her folds back a page of his magazine.

Soon they were driving down the dusty road past the little farms again. "Wait," the Senator said. "Slow down." They were approaching the house where they'd sat drinking cider, and out in the garden in front of the house was the young woman, hoeing. She stood up and leaned on her hoe and watched them go past as motionless and blank as the farmer and his cow had watched them go by in the opposite direction that morning. She didn't wave, or show any sign that they were anything but one more car boiling up dust to sift down over the leaves of her peas and zucchini and beans.

Damage Done by the Storm   63

The Senator looked at his grandson's face and saw that it wasn't necessary to ask. "You're nineteen," he said. The boy didn't say anything. "You brought me out here so you could have a good laugh at an old man admiring the ankles of the girl you've been visiting on your own?"

The Corolla rattled down a long narrow stretch of washboard gravel between banks of scrubby roadside brush. Nothing more was said between them for several minutes. "I'll be retiring soon," the Senator said, when they had pulled up before the Buckle house. "I'll have plenty of time for fishing, and little else to do that I can see."

But by the time he'd retired the boy had moved out to the Valley to live with the farmer's daughter. No more fishing trips had been offered, or two-man excursions of any other kind.

Judith had barely noticed, it seemed to him, when the boy left home. This was the way it ought to be, according to her. A mother raises her children and they leave. She gets on with things. "It is the same when you've raised your grandchildren, only the freedom is more precious for having been longer in coming." The Senator did not find this way of thinking easy to understand. There had been so many things he had wanted them to do together, he and the boy, when the demands of his work had made this impossible. Retired, he telephoned Warren daily, until she told him to stop. "The boy is too busy with his own life to make small talk with someone who has nothing to do."

"Sawmill." The woman facing him taps a finger against the window. "Nobody can work today. Just look at those drifts!"

The skeletons of trees are rigid as ironwork. A few have cracked open from the weight of snow, exposing the clean white wood within. The Senator looks at his watch. "We're slow."

Suddenly, this coach seems too hot, the air stale. He would walk, to exercise his cramped legs, but the aisle is filled with excited young skiers, their abandoned seats piled high with their outer clothing.

"I'm sure your grandson will understand," the woman says.

The young man beside her looks up from his magazine. "The only thing he can be sure of is that he'll be punished."

"Now you stop that," the woman says, in a gentle half-amused voice, as if this were her own small misbehaving child who must be corrected without being provoked to even worse. She looks out her window. "Sugar bush. Somebody's going to be surprised when they see what the storm's done to their shack." She offers mint candies out of a transparent bag, first to the boy beside her and then to the Senator. "A deer! Two deer!" Then, "Eeeeeeeeeee!"

Her mints spill onto the wet floor. The Senator's stomach also falls, the top of his head seems to lift. The border of skimpy trees has fallen away all at once, the ground has tilted suddenly and plunged to the bottom of a ravine. Slowing, they move out onto what must be a trestle, though nothing can be seen of it from the window. People stand to look: a deep chasm between walls of sharp wet stone, cushiony ledges of snow, the surface of a frozen river, solid and immobile, far below.

The chasm opens out into a wide valley. They can see, as if from the top of the snowy world, miles of buried scrub, white fields. Nothing moves – not a bird or car or single column of chimney smoke.

"Good lord," someone says. "We've stopped!"

The train is no longer moving. They sit suspended above the canyon.

"Just a tree blown down on the tracks, folks." The conductor moves down the aisle. "Please stay where you are. We think we'll be able to get it out of the way."

"So you say," says the young man facing the Senator. "If I were you I'd be up there looking for Jesse James!"

The conductor may not have heard. He seems to be making a count of bodies as he moves down the coach.

People speak in whispers. No one moves very much. One of the youthful skiers stands to take a picture but holds onto the back of his seat as if to help keep the train balanced.

The young man places his magazine on his lap and grins at the Senator. "We will now have a lesson in patience."

It seems to Senator Buckle that the youth, this boy, is altogether too pleased with himself, and for no discernible reason. "Life teaches us that," he replies. "Or tries to. This is more likely to be a lesson in tolerance, which is not quite the same." To the woman beside the youth he says, "If a train cannot guarantee to get you where you are going it should never have left in the first place."

"If that is what you call wisdom," the boy says, "you would be better to tell it to that fallen tree." The magazine on his lap is mostly coloured photos. Singers and musical bands, upside down from this angle, perform before inverted microphones.

"A chainsaw," says the woman, lifting her head as if her ears have just picked up some pleasant distant music.

To the Senator, it sounds as though the saw is working too hard. You can tell it has got its teeth into something too dense or too big for it. The saw squeals. Then it stalls, and has to be started again. No one can see the tree. No one knows how large it is. No one knows how long this will take.

"It's as if we're floating," someone says at a window.

"Why should we believe in that tree?" the boy says. "We sit here while Jesse James and his saw dismantle the trestle beneath us. We'll soon be falling to our deaths."

The idea seems to please him. He glances around as though hoping others have heard. It seems to give him pleasure to look the Senator in the eye and wink. Perhaps he thinks an old man spends most of his time contemplating death.

"Don't be a fool," the Senator says. "You will frighten the children."

In fact there are no children, that he can see. The excited skiers may be the youngest people on this train, and they seem delighted by this unexpected turn of events.

He cannot say the same for himself.

"You don't look well," the woman says. "Are you afraid of heights?"

"He's afraid of his grandson," the young man says. "He's afraid he'll be punished for being late."

"Ah," the woman says. She raises her ankle-locked boots and appears to be studying them for a moment, before returning them to the floor.

"Trains are sometimes late," the young man says, getting to his feet. "Whether you like it or not." He steps out into the aisle and starts toward the rear of the coach.

The woman watches the young man as far as the toilet door. To the Senator she says, "Your grandson will understand," she says. "Even when we're sure that we've failed, we have to be grateful we're not those poor folks who've lost the chance to try."

He assumes she means those who have lost their children. "Even a close call can drive you crazy."

The woman's raised eyebrows invite more. She has a broad,

ruddy, motherly sort of face that suggests there isn't a thing you could say that she hasn't heard before.

The Senator lowers his voice. "I'm thinking of a camping trip I'll never forget."

This was at a time when their daughter and the boy's father were having trouble in their marriage. Warren and his sister had been sent east for a holiday. He remembers Warren as a round-eyed little kid, one of those white-haired children, still at that stage where the head seems too big for the body. "One day we stopped for a picnic on the side of a quiet road and the boy went across to pee in the bushes." The Senator – who was not a senator yet, but still a cabinet minister – watched him cross the pavement. He was wearing short pants and a red-and-white striped T-shirt, a strip of bare flesh showing in the gap. "I looked up from the camp stove and saw him start back across the road at the same moment I heard a truck coming over the rise."

"Uh oh," the woman says.

He can't tell her all of this. Something in his brain did the figuring for him – he knew they were going to meet. The boy would go up in the air, he'd land on the roof of the truck, and slide off onto the gravel shoulder a broken mess. The truck was coming at sixty or seventy miles an hour; he didn't have a chance. Alfred Buckle yelled. If the boy stopped where he was, he might be saved. But the name – the name that came out of his mouth wasn't the boy's. It was his sister's name. The boy kept coming.

Buckle tried to find the name but could not. His brain, it seemed, had frozen.

Nothing had stopped, the truck was still coming, maybe the driver hadn't even seen the boy – while this man's stubborn tongue refused to obey.

Hodgins-Damage.pages   6/22/04   3:11 PM   Page 68

It is too hot in here. He rests his head against the cool glass of the window. Again and again the boy must be saved, even now. Awake, asleep. God knows how many nights it has happened since then, exactly the same, the wrong name forcing itself up his throat. I must stop him, I must stop him, but cannot.

He can tell the woman this much: "The boy stopped on the centre line as if that were his goal all along, and the truck went rocketing past within inches of him. He hadn't even known it was coming! Now, of course, he couldn't move. He stood where he was, bawling, while I went out to carry him back to the car."

Despising himself for having space in his head to think, *How would I have told his parents? How could I have faced them? How could I have lived afterwards?*

How often he's had to relive this, has had to stick with it until he was sure that this time he got the name right, and the boy could hear him and stop before it was too late.

"If only we could always be so sure that we aren't needed!" the woman says, apparently delighted to have heard something in the story the Senator has missed.

This is a talent she apparently has in common with Judith, who seems capable of seeing something in every situation that he has entirely missed. It is because he is so self-absorbed, she says. It is because he has found nothing in retirement to keep him alert and sensitive to the complications in people. It is because he refuses to socialize with those still active in political life, having discovered how frustrating it is to have no say in matters, how tempting it is to sound off to those who would rather not listen. Judith has her own tendency to lecture, as if she were still in the classroom, and no end of suggestions for a man who has walked out into unfamiliar territory.

There is no "unfamiliar territory" in that recurring dream. His roadside failure has had its echoes in a hundred later instances. A grandfather absorbed in public life could not always live up to the private expectations of the boy who sat across the table from him every morning for most of his growing-up years. Fortunately there were no more speeding trucks, but there were concerts missed, holidays cancelled, and promises forgotten, all in the cause of the Nation's Business.

After a few angry groans from that chainsaw, there is sudden quiet. Everyone inside the train hushes. When the conductor starts down the aisle again, faces turn up to him. "We'll soon be moving again, folks. We've just about got that tree out of our way."

The woman facing the Senator informs the conductor that the young fellow who was sitting beside her hasn't returned from the toilet. "Maybe someone ought to check. He was rather pale."

"The toilet?" the conductor says. "The door's open." He checks, but there is no one inside.

"That's strange," the woman says. "There isn't anywhere else that he could –!" Again, her cry draws attention to herself. She is looking out her window at the face of the rusty-haired youth, who is looking in at the Senator through the glass, upside down.

The inverted mouth is saying something they can't hear. One arm swings down and presses a hand against the glass. The lines of the palm are a startling red, as if they've been traced over with ink from a marking pen.

The conductor rushes out the back door and another man in uniform comes thumping down the coach to follow him. It is hardly possible to believe such a thing but now the young man is sticking out his tongue. He crosses his eyes, he thumbs his nose, he laughs. All of this at Senator Alfred Buckle. "Because he knows you can't do a thing to stop him," says the woman across from him. The young man puts both thumbs in his ears and flaps his fingers.

"Maybe he's an acrobat," someone says.

Another: "What keeps him from falling?"

"If we refuse to look," the woman says. "If there's no one to put on a show for –"

But he is putting on his show for Senator Buckle, that is clear. There are all these others trapped behind the glass but it is the Senator he is looking at. What does he think he can see? The youth's gestures are directed at someone he imagines he can see in the Senator, upside down inside the glass, unable to do a thing.

Suddenly he isn't there. Just like that. You are looking at a face and then it is gone. The Senator's stomach clenches as it does when an elevator drops too suddenly. Startled cries fill the coach.

People leap up, pressing faces to the windows. There is nothing to see below but the snow and ice and a few bare peaks of rock. Has a wind carried him under the trestle to be caught in the timbers, or has the ice opened up just long enough to swallow him and then closed? There is nothing below to tell you he ever existed. Just ice, and all that blank impassive snow.

"He went *up*," says the woman. She smiles as if she has pulled it off herself. "He was snatched up, he didn't fall. It was just so fast, if you weren't exactly looking –"

"Up?" The Senator can't make the word mean anything.

"He was rescued from above," the woman says. "They snatched him up, I suppose, by the ankles."

"Who was he?" someone says. Faces turn to Senator Buckle, as if he should know. Why would a man make faces at someone if there weren't something between them? Has the old man said something that caused him to hang upside down above the abyss? Is there something the boy saw that the others could not?

The conductor and his assistant receive a round of applause as they escort their man down the aisle. Both of the rescuers' faces are grim. Only the rescued one is smiling. He seems to believe he is being returned to his seat, and starts to fold his knees. But the conductor has other plans and propels him down through the coach, down past the applause, to the door. Maybe they have a special room for maniacs.

The woman offers the Senator a smile. "Maybe you should put your head between your knees."

He is the only one still on his feet. "Wait," he says. Though his head is light, his vision blurred, he starts after the conductor.

But the conductor turns and blocks the door. "Better go back to your seat, sir. We'll be leaving now."

"Just let me talk to him."

The conductor's face is not a friendly one. "We'll take care of him, don't worry."

"Let him explain himself." The Senator is aware that his voice has slipped into a higher register – strained, reined-in, furiously patient. "Let him come back and tell me what he meant."

"Go back to your friends," the conductor says, gathering all his authority into his voice. "You don't want us to take you into custody as well."

The Senator waits only long enough for the door to close before slamming his fist against the wall. Lightning shards of pain shoot up his arm. Doubled over, his hand between his knees, he waits for something in his swimming head to calm down. When he has returned to his seat, he keeps his hand where the woman can't see. He stretches his fingers, bends them. Nothing has been broken.

"They'll phone ahead for someone to meet him at the next stop," the woman says. She settles back and leans her head against the glass. "Obviously he isn't well, he should not be travelling alone. It is impossible to know what may be going on inside the most ordinary-looking strangers." They click along the tracks past a bank of snow-laden bushes, gradually gaining speed. The woman is apparently absorbed in thought, looking out the window.

The Senator rests his head against the glass and closes his eyes. Judith will have completed any number of tasks by now. By now she will have spoken to any number of people, convincing them to contribute time or money to one of her arts charities. Invitations to her March Break-up party will have been addressed and, possibly, mailed. She will eventually have had one of her light lunches, no doubt e-mailing at the same time, the minutes of a recent meeting on her newly purchased computer. If the buses are running, she will quite likely be on her way to visit Betty Borleski in the hospital.

He will be late for the ribbon-cutting, late for the speeches. The converted mill will be filled already with neighbours, friends, farmers from the surrounding area, looking through the wooden toys and wax spiral candles and hand-painted calendars and braided rugs, stuffing the till with their money, offering young Warren and the woman he lives with their congratulations for the imagination and hard work they had put into this project. Bottles of wine will have been opened. Where machines once trembled and belts turned creaking shafts for grinding flour, another free-enterprise venture has been launched in the world.

Outside, icicles as thick as an arm reach from the eaves down to the surface of the frozen stream, where a water wheel once turned for someone else's dream.

Warren's sister will not be there, of course, having run off a year ago to New Orleans, with a trumpet player named – good lord! – Bernie DeWitt.

Warren will be smiling, charming everyone, busy serving wine when he isn't working the till, but he will not be too busy to notice that his grandfather hasn't shown up. It is possible that he is wondering, at this moment, if he could really expect the Senator's face to appear at the door, exercising his right to be let inside and treated as though he belonged. It is not entirely impossible, the Senator thinks, that when he has finally got off this train and walked to the village centre, he could even find the boy standing in the doorway waiting to welcome him.

THE DROVER'S WIFE

For years she was known as Hard-hearted Hazel in the logging camps up and down the coast of British Columbia. She was also known as Hazel Haulback, Highball Hazel, and The Terror of the Woods. Government inspectors trembled at the thought of visiting her outfit. She had little time for critics. One civil servant found fault with her safety record and discovered how clumsy she could be while bringing his piping hot soup to the table. When a government forester arrived with plans for replacing her felled trees with tiny seedlings that would eventually become second-growth fir, she didn't let him off the dock. She blocked his way with her own substantial body and stared him down. When she learned that his name was Cyrus Drysdale, she let loose her fiercest Australian invective, and even though he insisted he was not related to the famous Aussie painter with that surname, she tilted him into the salt chuck. Subsequent inspectors sometimes wrote their reports without leaving their boats.

That my client has an enduring reputation in the Antipodes would be unknown to me still if I had not been thumbing through a library book and come upon a reproduction of Sir Russell Drysdale's painting titled *The Drover's Wife*. This famous image, depicting a large woman with a suitcase standing at the forefront of a flat barren landscape (the horizon broken only by a distant horse and wagon amongst a clutch of dead scraggly trees) was familiar to me during the dozen years I was married to an Australian and living in Katoomba. What struck me this time was the remarkable resemblance to the woman who'd recently become my client here in Victoria – that pretty face, those big bones, those sturdy legs. The accompanying text, a complaint by a certain Dr. Bail, insists that the woman was not the drover's wife at all, as the title of the painting suggests, but his *own* wife. Further, this dentist accuses his wife of leaving him and their two children in order to run off with the owner of that horse and wagon. Noticing her physical resemblance to the accused woman, I thought it might be amusing to show the reproduction to my client.

She was not even slightly amused. She swore loudly, as she'd become accustomed to doing in the logging camps. "Bloody hell! That bastard kept me standing in the heat for hours while he fiddlearsed with his damn canvas. By the time he let me go, Danny-boy was ropeable. 'Who d'you think you are,' he says, 'the Queen of bloody Sheba? Get busy and start me tea!'" After studying the picture a little longer, she had some complaints of her own. "Where's the sweat on me neck? Where's the flies on me lip? Where's the bloody *sheep*?" Apparently this was the first time she'd seen the painting.

To me she admitted to feeling some sympathy for Dr. Bail, though she claimed he was never much of a dentist. In fact she blames him for the fact that she no longer has a tooth of her own in her head. "Comes from trusting an incompetent fool just because you married him!" She did not explain why she left him, however, or why she eventually left the drover as well, or how it was that she came to cross the Pacific.

I met Hazel when she called my business number, as do many seniors in this city when they've discovered a need for my services. Often it is the son or daughter of the elderly who calls for my help – a son or daughter living far away, that is – but in this case it was the eighty-seven-year-old woman herself who telephoned, having decided it was time to give up her townhouse and move to a seniors complex where, as she put it, "some other poor sod can cook my meals for a change."

My own mother was in her greatest need while I was half a world away in Katoomba. It nearly drove me crazy making arrangements from that distance – finding a good nursing home, investigating government agencies, finding someone to move her belongings and sell off the junk she no longer needed. After my marriage failed and I came home to Victoria, I discovered a large population of seniors living here, many of them having retired from elsewhere, leaving sons and daughters and all other relatives behind. It occurred to me that I might make a living doing for others what I wish someone had done for me. Thus "Rent-a-Rellie" was born.

Of course when Hazel first called me she did not admit to having "rellies" already. She certainly didn't mention two daughters in Adelaide. In fact, she said she had no living family at all, but, to put it her way, she sure as shootin' needed someone like me to find her a decent place to live, before she began to forget who the hell she was.

At first I didn't realize who she was. That is, I didn't know she was the Hazel Bailey of local legend until some time during one of our drives to visit retirement homes. At her advanced age, it is possible that half the people who pass her on the street, though aware of the story of her life in this province, would not know who they were looking at. That is, they would not recognize the woman who, half a lifetime ago, is believed to have appeared from "nowhere" and, after a long night of drinking at the Kick and Kill in the village of Port Annie, accompanied Shorty Maclean up past Desolation Sound to the little gyppo logging outfit he managed for a Vancouver company.

Rusted old equipment. Leaking shacks hanging at various angles over the sea. Shorty was felling trees off hillsides steeper than a doghouse roof. Giant firs came toppling to earth before Hazel's eyes, as broad across the trunk as that drover's wagon. When she ventured into the rain forest for the first time, brushing aside the boughs of hemlock and hanging swatches of old man's beard, she felt, she said, like a flea in the hairy armpit of some stupendous beast.

For most new arrivals, the temptation is to marvel at these soaring giants, this green luxurious growth. But Hazel's first thought, she told me, was to marvel at the amount of work there was to be done if this place was ever to look like the uncluttered flat approach to Ayers Rock. Cedar trunks blocked the view. Ferns and salal and Oregon grape grew up those sturdy legs, it seemed, even as she stood looking. "A bloomin' jungle from here to buggery," she said, speaking as I am sure she would never have spoken as the wife of an Adelaide dentist. "Someone's gotta clear this so's a bloke can *see*."

We don't know how long it took before she saw that she herself was the someone who would eventually clear it all. At first she cooked for the bunkhouse men. She repaired the leaking roofs. In the evenings she also played a little poker. Within the year she'd scraped together enough winnings to buy a piece of the company – a large enough piece, apparently, to give her the power to serve

Shorty Maclean his walking papers the first time he contradicted an order. Hazel ran the show her way. Nobody offered advice. She had discovered, she said, that it wasn't the dentist that she'd been running from, or the drover, but the whole idea of letting someone else run the show. She'd always wanted to be the biggest thing in the picture. "He called it my silly streak," she said, referring to the dentist. "But it was just that once in a while I forgot myself and behaved as though the world was meant for me to live in too."

If she wanted to be the biggest thing in the picture, she saw that her opportunity had arrived. She also saw there was plenty of picture to fill. No one who needed the work dared to comment on her style of going about it, even when she took to chewing tobacco and spitting off to the side like the rest of the crew. She put on a great deal of weight, much of it muscle. If one of the men was sick, she set chokers or ran the yarding machine in his stead. The only times she wore a dress was when one or another of the boys was killed in a logging accident and she was obliged to attend – and sometimes conduct – the funeral.

She ran such a highball outfit that it wasn't long before she was making enough profit to start buying up other small companies working those woods. She was so surprised to have her orders obeyed by all these men, including tall Swedes who bragged of wrestling with grizzlies, that she got a little carried away with her power. She wanted to boss the whole coast.

She very nearly succeeded. By the time she'd become the owner of the third largest private timber company in the province, men in positions of authority were asking her to enter politics. She refused. There were still too many trees standing, too many places where you couldn't *see*. Once she'd got started, it seemed she couldn't stop. Of course she never quite succeeded in making British Columbia look like the Nullarbor Plain, but she came about as close as it is possible to come. When Highball Hazel and her boys had been through, whole mountainsides and valleys looked like the shaved scalps of lice-ridden kids. You could *see* all right, but never very far – mountains got in the way. And what you could see tended to look like a ravaged battlefield just after an invading army had gone through.

By the time she sold out to an American firm, she had discarded or worn out or otherwise outlasted three more men she referred to as her "de facto" husbands. She invested her fortune in the high-tech industries and wandered up and down the coast, one of the wealthiest people in the province, wondering what to do with the rest of her life. Checking the stock market daily was hardly enough for an active woman like her. "All I wanted was to carve me out a place where I could fit," she said. She did not consider returning to Adelaide.

Her former acquaintances in Australia would probably be amused to learn that, after her retirement, she became a drover's wife once again. A drover's wife and a drover herself as well. She filled me in on a few details from this chapter of her life over lunch in the dining room of the Dogwood Manor. She has kept her true identity from the other residents, having registered with her birth name. "These old birds'd mess their Pampers if they knew who's living amongst them. Hell, I reckon most of them have never even been in the same room as someone like me."

One rainy afternoon during her period of purposeless life and indecision, she'd been once again sitting over a beer in the Kick and Kill with some old drinking buddies. "My foul mood wasn't because of the rain, which I'd got used to, but because I'd gone and found myself thinking about those two girls I left in

Adelaide." She imagined them as mothers themselves by now, wondering whatever happened to the woman they only vaguely remembered. Did they wonder why she'd run off with the drover, or imagine that she had then run off with the man who'd painted her portrait that hot afternoon? She was on the verge of deciding to write the dentist for information about them when a man sat down across the table and waited for her to notice him.

She not only noticed him, she recognized him. This was the government reforester she'd tossed in the drink. Cyrus Drysdale.

His glare was as fierce as hers, and fuelled with as much dislike. He'd spent his lifetime planting seedlings to replace the trees she'd been cutting down. He knew by now that he'd lost the battle, at least in this part of the world.

"Improved your breaststroke yet?" she said, remembering his frantic efforts to get back to his boat.

"I heard you'd given up," he said.

When he could see that his choice of language was unfortunate (she'd clenched a fist), he rephrased it. "Retired, that is. Withdrawn your services from the industry that has brought so much wealth to this province."

"And what have *you* got to show for your efforts?" she said.

He confessed he had very little to show. In *his* retirement he had become involved in the environmental movement. Poisonous chemicals were still being used to kill the wild underbrush that grew so fast that it choked off the seedlings, preventing them from becoming timber for future generations to fell. Poisonous chemicals were not, he said, environmentally sound. Fish died. Deer died. Herds of elk were dying. "Those, that is, that hadn't already died when their habitats were ruined by people like yourself. If you'll forgive my saying so."

At first she pushed away and took her drink to another table and sat with her back to him. But it wasn't in her to let someone else have the last word. After a few minutes she came back and sat across from Cyrus Drysdale again and said, "What do you mean – fish dying?"

"Maybe my brain was going a little soft," she told me. "I found myself thinking again about my girls in South Australia. How would they feel if they heard their mother was responsible for the extinction of the magnificent elk?"

"Hell, Cyrus," she eventually said, "this shouldn't be a problem for a couple of tough old crustaceans like us." By this time she was talking like a true West Coaster.

They drank in silence for a few minutes, each searching the bottom of a beer glass for inspiration. When Hazel saw what could be an answer to the problem, a few more minutes passed while she considered whether to share it. He was, after all, her old enemy.

"I'll go to my grave a failure," Drysdale said. "Anyone travelling up this coast will see that I've wasted my life."

It wasn't pity that caused her to share her inspiration. It was the sudden recognition that she could be looking at a whole new way of making herself the biggest thing in the picture. If they made a success of it, she would contact those abandoned girls and make them proud of her. "You're trying to get away from using chemicals on the woody-weeds?" she said. "One thing I learned during a life on another continent is that a certain dumb beast will chew just about anything right to the nub if you let 'em. The stupid merinos draggin' themselves around the dust down the Riverina would think they'd gone to heaven if they saw what we can offer! How many can we get our hands on fast?"

Cyrus Drysdale stared at her for a few minutes, trying to absorb what she'd told him. He had not realized until that moment, he later admitted to others, what a beautiful woman she was, despite her remarkable size. "And smart too. And, thank God, as stubborn as anyone's mule. Once she gets something into her head you couldn't stop her with a tank."

Within months they were partners operating a company that brought truckloads of sheep from farmers east of the Rocky Mountains and set them loose on the coastal mountainsides. A few months into their first season, Hazel and Cyrus were moving from mountain to mountain up and down the coast. They lived in a tent. You could come upon them around a bend in the road, or up the shadowy silence of some narrow inlet, camped on the edge of a clear-cut: two aging shepherds sitting inside their tent out of the rain, watching their flock nibble its way up slopes once scalped by Highball Hazel's outfit. Chewing the weeds so the planted seedlings could grow.

She claims she was happy as Cyrus Drysdale's companion. A journalist from the *Vancouver Sun* visited them long enough to take a photo for the Saturday second-front page. Hazel in her rain-gear stood mountainous amongst the stumps and seedlings, filling half the space, while Cyrus laboured to secure the tent pegs in the background. In the distance, sheep were chewing their way up a neighbouring canyon crowded with the tasty leaves of rapidly growing young alder.

By the end of the season, unfortunately, Hazel and Cyrus had not yet found a way to iron out a small glitch they'd discovered in their system: the task of teaching these animals the difference between weeds and future timber. They didn't know whether this

defect was particular to the breed of sheep or common to the
entire species. Expert animal trainers were called in, including
one famous for his handling of Hollywood dogs. True success, it
seemed, might depend upon someone developing a genetically
altered breed of sheep allergic to evergreens. When most of the
woolly beasts were still resisting instruction a year later, the part-
nership began to suffer from the strain. Apparently people in the
mountain town of Goat Leg speak even now of the evening in
which the private tension between man and woman entered the
public domain.

Naturally it began as a competition in blame. It was *her* fault
for suggesting the sheep in the first place. It was *his* fault for being
so eager to please her, just to gain access to her bed. It was
undoubtedly *her* intention all along to draw him into a foolish
scheme that would mock his efforts to save the environment.
It was undoubtedly *his* intention from the beginning to make
fools of the most important animal in her country of origin. "I
should've bloody drowned you when I had the chance."

This was in Goat Leg's *Glorious Hangover Pub*. At five o'clock
the place was crowded with local loggers, farmers, and tree-
planters exchanging their own grumbled dissatisfactions through
their smoke and fumes.

"You are a destroyer," Drysdale shouted. "You destroy forests,
you destroy rules and laws, you destroy men. I believe those sheep
are not real sheep at all." And here he spluttered a bit, trying to
find the right words. "Those sheep are the evil servants of your
wicked mind."

Men lined up at the telephone to invite wives and sweethearts down to witness what they sensed would be a battle worth

recalling for their grandchildren. What had started out as a "holy row" was beginning to look like the run-up to a murder. "The poor little bastard don't have a snowball's chance."

The battle might have fizzled out before the wives and sweethearts had put on their lipstick if a local logger named Howie Black hadn't decided to out-shout the squabbling pair. Still nursing the bitter memory of being fired by Hazel Haulback fifteen years before ("I don't like your ugly face," she'd said. "Get it out of my sight before I alter it"), he was further insulted that she'd failed to recognize him seated at the nearest table. "Take your racket somewheres else," he said. "The pair of youse are curdling my beer." In the silence that followed, he added for the benefit of the room, "Oh, how the mighty have fallen, eh boys? From boss-lady over a bloody army of men she's gone to babysitting a herd of stupid sheep. Some people don't have no pride."

And here is where we must relinquish any doubts about Hazel's Australian origins, or her time as a dentist's companion. Her first husband could not have removed a half-dozen teeth any faster. When Howie Black's head snapped back from the fist to his jaw, his front teeth dropped, one after another, tinkling, into several people's drinks. Once Black had been put out of commission, Hazel turned on Cyrus Drysdale with a sound her former countrymen would no doubt have recognized as an Aboriginal war cry and a tackle that had its choreographical roots in Australian Rules footie. No pub in Alice Springs is likely to have seen so many pieces of furniture broken in a single dust-up.

Eventually Hazel sold out to Cyrus Drysdale and, consistent with the pattern of her life, walked out on him. Drysdale tried to make a go of it, but eventually he gave up the business as well, selling to a pair of young entrepreneurs who were determined to make this environmentally friendly enterprise work. I understand this company is at present trying to find an inexpensive way of renting genuine Down Under sheep for a few months of each year. Perhaps they believe that sheep from the dusty plains of western New South Wales will be so overjoyed to see all that unfamiliar green, so grateful for the soft veined leaves of the new alders, that they will turn up their noses at the acidic needles of the tiny firs and hemlock.

When Hazel walked out on Drysdale, she did not, for a change, leave with another man. She moved down here to the capital city, and lived alone in her townhouse until – these several years later – she moved to the assisted care home I'd helped her to find. This elderly woman, sturdy enough even now, though weighing little more than half her former weight, was hard of hearing, dim of sight, and not too successful at hiding the tremor in her hands. Sitting across the dining-room table from her, I imagined her fellow residents would find it difficult to believe she'd once been known as Hard-hearted Hazel, The Terror of the Woods.

Perhaps she sensed my thought. She slapped a sudden hand on the table and lowered her voice to a growl. "I keep expecting that bugger to show up in here." By the way her gaze darted fiercely about, I assumed that "here" was this dining room, deserted by everyone but us. "Sooner or later he's going to call and ask you to find him a place."

"And?" I said, knowing that "the bugger" would have to be Cyrus Drysdale. "You want me to take him elsewhere – right? There are lots of care homes in this city."

"Hell no, that's not what I meant!" she roared. "Bring him here! Just because I'm old don't mean I've run out of steam." She lowered her voice, perhaps in case an administrator was hiding behind one of the pillars. "By now most of that land I cleared has grown up again with new timber, thanks to the seedlings he planted after my crew had gone through. I want to see the look on the son of a bitch's face when I tell him I'm thinking of busting outta here and taking up logging again, make a second fortune off them trees he planted. That oughta start a battle good enough to last till one of us is carted off to the morgue. What I can't stand is the thought of dyin' of boredom."

I might have thought that a woman with Hazel's memories was unlikely to die of boredom, but she was clearly a woman who needed to scheme and anticipate and carry out new conquests, even at this late stage of her life.

We may certainly feel sorry for the grief Hazel has caused Dr. Bail and the daughters she never got around to contacting, as well as for the mysterious drover she referred to as "Danny-boy." But if she is not the drover's wife, as Dr. Murray Bail insists, she can hardly be considered Bail's wife either, after all this time, nor the wife of several other men who once believed she belonged to them. Hazel has never belonged to anyone. I understand there is a good deal of sympathy in Australia for the figure Hazel cuts in the famous painting – an unhappy woman, dependent upon the wishes of a man while at the mercy of a harsh environment. Those who see in that young Hazel the symbol of a female victim would, I imagine, be heartened to learn that she succeeded in altering her destiny once she arrived on these shores. Look to the legs. She was never meant to be toppled.

GALLERIES

Anyone seeing them would say "mother and son" right away – freckles and pale ginger hair told everything. He knew this. People coming in to this converted cotton warehouse and seeing them at their salad plates would guess immediately that this slim talkative woman with the dramatic hand gestures was related to the unsmiling young man across the table. And that they were tourists – Faulkner tourists.

He hated it, that strangers could guess this about him so quickly. What kind of thirty-year-old travelled with his mother? To any of these Mississippi diners and waiters they could be one of those mother-and-son teams you saw at the opera, when in fact they never went anywhere together back home. In Edmonton his mother preferred to work day and night on her precious book. While for him there was Dorothy to go places with. After a week of typing speeches in a legislature office, Dorothy Schmidt liked to be taken to movies set in the romantic past, and to sit afterwards over a coffee where she would pretend to consider his proposal.

Of course Dorothy was not here. Just the two of them were here, two tourists sitting across from one another like this at every meal. His mother was the one who felt it was necessary that they talk.

He didn't always listen, nor especially avoid listening either. As his mother spoke about her day's discoveries he watched their waitress, a lively young woman with skin as close as skin could possible come to being black. Burnt-almond chocolate was what he thought of. And felt a sort of small shock in the pit of his stomach when she turned to walk away with that high hip-tilting walk.

He'd pretended to misunderstand much of the menu, in order to give himself the opportunity to hear her talk: "Don' know what that is? Lord – you pullin' ma leg!" It had been his suspicion that the accent they'd been hearing in this state was put on for their benefit. His mother objected to this: "Don't be silly. If you were to *read* you'd know that's the way they talk."

Yet she seemed to find the waitress as interesting as he did. "Have you noticed? When she's not busy running with plates up her arm she's parked up there at the counter, studying. I recognize the book she's reading."

"What else do you expect waitresses to be doing in a university town?" he said.

He hoped his sarcasm might discourage her, but of course knew better. She considered herself to hold some sort of proprietorship over everything here.

She could hardly wait for the young woman to come back with the coffee pot. "None for me." She put out a hand and barely touched the waitress's arm. "But I couldn't help noticing. I once taught from that same anthology." She laced her freckled hands together beneath her chin and looked up with expectation – pleased in advance.

The waitress cocked her hip and planted one fist against it while she poured coffee into his cup. "Exam tomorrow. I ain't finished the damn thing yet! *As I Lay Dyin'*s got me stalled."

"Good heavens!" His mother threw herself against the back of her chair. "We were, just this afternoon – weren't we, Gordon? – we drove down there, the Yocana River. Just about where old Anse Bundren must have tried getting that coffin across."

Of course it hadn't exactly been in flood today – a disappointment. Just a slow trickle of yellow mud.

"My mother's working on a book about the author," he explained. "In case there aren't already enough of them out there that nobody will ever read."

"Yeah? Well, I heard that story supposed to be someplace 'round here. They tell me he's pretty big stuff, but that don't mean nothin' to me – I come from twenty mile up the road."

His mother clapped her hands. "Twenty miles! While we – how far have we come?"

Of course they hadn't come here directly, but had flown right down to New Orleans, where she had looked up some of the Great Author's early haunts. Then they'd driven up the river. Oxford must be approached slowly, she believed, and from the south – not descended upon suddenly from the northern air.

"Reading about her own neighbours and not knowing it!" his mother said, when the waitress had moved on to other tables. Apparently this proved something about the girl, who could not recognize the very world that had been created for her to walk around in.

When the waitress returned, his mother told her how they'd driven in to the Faulkner home today at noon, as soon as they'd arrived in town, and discovered a sign on the front door saying the house was closed for the season. She'd been outraged. After coming all this way! "And then, we heard this fluttering inside. A bird was trapped in the house. A small brown wide-mouthed bird, which kept flinging itself at the window and getting caught up in the curtains. We went off and found a bookstore downtown and reported the bird – and earned ourselves a private tour of the house." She paused, and looked at him. "Which my son here declined, in favour of lounging in the shade."

When the waitress came back with his receipt and his change on a plastic tray, she paused, looked at him a moment, and said, "Y'all come back now – hear?" precisely as every waitress and store clerk north of Baton Rouge had said it, though none of the others had looked at him quite this way, or winked.

It was a look he would like to have captured on film, to take home and think about later. But even if such a thing were possible, he'd all but given up taking photographs since they'd entered this state. His mother had raised such objections every time he lifted his Pentax that he'd decided to put it out of temptation's way in the trunk of the rented Honda.

In Louisiana things had been different. She'd encouraged him. But in Louisiana she'd been a tourist. In Mississippi she'd become a pilgrim. As soon as they'd crossed the state line his camera became as vulgar and inappropriate as it might have been at a private audience with the Dalai Lama, say, or inside the Forbidden City. "I'd just rather you didn't. People have feelings." Not even a row of small children sitting in a ditch were to be insulted by the click of a camera shutter. Nor were the old slow stuttering gas station attendant and his lounging cohorts to be offended. "They'll think you consider them quaint." She'd nearly had a fit when he'd wanted to photograph a narrow street of unpainted

shacks in Natchez, where black families spilled out over the col-
lapsing furniture on their front verandas. "Slave shacks," he'd
said. She'd slapped the camera down out of sight. "You want one
of them to come after us with a knife?"

Why not? The prizes he'd won for his photography were not
the result of capturing the beautiful or the exotic or even the
provocative with his camera. He was praised for his ability to *surprise*, to discover the unexpected in the midst of the merely pic-
turesque. Judges said he caught life unawares. It was his habit to
snap dozens of pictures of a place that fascinated him – usually for
reasons he didn't understand – and then afterwards to pore over
them all until he found a small sign of unexpected life in some
corner, looking as if it were just about to leap out and attack you
for your impertinence. A little boy you hadn't consciously
noticed, taking a leak by a tree. The offended face of a cat, glaring
down from behind a screen of leaves. Sometimes your instincts
could surprise the world – find things you hadn't been aware of.
His mother knew about his scatter-gun approach. He suspected
she just didn't want him surprising any unexpected life up out of a
landscape she thought she knew everything about already,
though all that she knew she'd got from books. *Faulkner's* books.

The smells of honeysuckle and wisteria in this heavy May
heat apparently gave everything here the sacred aura of some
holy place. *He* had known that smell. *He* may have driven this
road in his Rambler. *He* may have stopped for pipe tobacco at
that tilted country store. Tension mounted as they drove north
into pine country. It was for this – her childlike wonder, not the
determined research – that he was prepared to bow to her unrea-
sonable attitude toward his camera. For this, and for the edge-of-
hysteria state she'd lived in since his father's death, he'd agreed to

come along on her trip at a time when he should have been at
home in Edmonton studying for his civil-service exam.

Their grey brick house stood on a street that was itself still grey
from the residue of winter. There had been a few dull heaps of
still unrotted snow beneath some of the trees when they'd left.
Yet he would have preferred, now, to be there. Without his
camera he found this place to have less interest for him than a
televised travelogue.

For her it became more real every minute that it lived up to
her expectations. During the morning, he'd driven her out into
the country to find some crossroads village that was supposed to
have served as a model for Frenchman's Bend in the novels. It
was a warm day, sweet-smelling, with insects screeching in the
trees. She insisted he park across the road from the general store
while she went inside. She stayed so long that he began to
worry, expecting the driver of some passing pickup to stop and
challenge his right to be here. Some backwoods redneck. But
then a long-legged long-necked farmer came by, with a suit
jacket pulled over his overalls, and walked up the steps to the
store. Apparently this was what she'd been waiting for. She
came out, soon after that, and said, "He could have been a cousin
to Flem Snopes." And seemed to have been freed, in some way, to
go on.

On the second day, while she visited the university library's
special room, with its cabinets of first editions and glass cases of
awards and photographs and scrapbooks of clippings, he walked
downtown to find a postcard for Dorothy. A Southern Belle
standing with a parasol beneath a magnolia tree. This would

appeal to her love of the romance in history. "Haven't been lynched yet," he wrote when he'd returned to sit on the library steps. "Haven't been beaten up by any pig-eyed sheriffs." She had seen television dramas, and warned him to keep his mouth shut. She believed the woods to be swarming with furious African Americans, slobbering hillbillies, and vicious Klanners. What good would his proposal of marriage do her then, she said, if he got himself strung up for offending people?

She'd sat on his proposal for more than a year, and would listen to no talk of experimental cohabitation. To tell the truth, he wasn't all that anxious any more to get an answer from her. He supposed some part of him still hoped that life might yet offer up a surprise. Or perhaps he only believed he ought to hope for such a thing.

"This gal in the photo asked me to marry her," he wrote, "and live with her on her daddy's plantation." He bit the end of the pen. What did you write to someone like Dorothy?

"Your Momma so worked up about ol' Bill that she went and evaporated?" Last night's waitress stood at the foot of the steps with her arms about a load of books. She threw up a laugh to the cedars.

"You pass that exam?"

"Finished it, is all I can say." She shrugged, kept looking off this way and that even as she was talking to him. "What do I know about fire and flood?" Her gaze came rolling around and across the front of the library above his head and down to nail him solid where he sat. "You write books like your Momma?"

"I write letters for a Member of the Alberta Legislature – to his constituents. Telling them how much he appreciates their complaints."

"You mean, when you're not someone else's chauffeur you're someone else's voice?"

"It's a job. One day I'll be promoted to a better one."

"Boredom must be why you travel then. Ammo travel too someday." She sat on the step beside him and hugged her books to her chest. "Want to see N'awlins. Want to see ol' Elvis' place up there in Memphis. Want to see Chicago!"

"I must've taken a million photos in New Orleans. Caught a musician shaking trombone spit into the trumpeter's drink."

"Where's your camera now? You think we don't have nothing to take pictures of?"

"Locked in the trunk of that little white car," he said. "She doesn't like it when I take photos of Mississippi. She thinks it ought to be left alone."

She looked at him as if she couldn't make up her mind whether to be shocked or amused. "Son, how come you so big for twelve years old?"

No son was ever more than twelve years old, he might have said. "She was off looking into some old papers in Virginia a year ago when my father died, suddenly, back home, and she never quite got over it. She's edgy. But she seems to think there's some kind of race to get this book finished. She thinks she's competing with the others. I tag along. And drive."

She watched clusters of students cross the grass and go into one or another of the buildings. "What's stopping you from taking pictures now? Look at all them trees. That blonde up yonder looks your type."

"Nothing here I want to take pictures of."

"What you want then?"

"Shacks and mansions. Black faces, old faces, kids' faces. All those cabins you see out along the country roads, with chairs and iceboxes on their porches, and kids all over the steps, and car bodies buried in weeds. Where I come from you don't see people living as if the outside's same as the inside – they wouldn't last long if they did."

There were verandas on the houses of his street in Edmonton, he told her, but they were mostly unused, or glassed-in and converted to tiny solariums. There, the verandas were buffer zones, shielding the house's privacy from passersby; here they seemed more like theatre stages where everything was set out to be seen by whoever happened by.

She waited through this explanation with a smile. "Whoa!" She laughed. "You go tell your Momma you're drivin' this woman home. I'm tired from that exam and don't want to sit on no bus."

He looked hard, to see if she meant it. It seemed that she did. "She'll be in there for hours," he said.

Driving north through pine forest, he could scarcely think of anything to say to her. She had little to say herself. She had no opinion of her university classes. She knew nothing about the people who lived in the tidy white houses on either side of the road. She seemed uninterested in discovering anything about his own home. When he mentioned that the man he worked for had been elected by people in a corner of the province close to Montana, she watched out the window for a long while as if she hadn't heard. Then she said, "Don't know nobody's been to Alberta yet, but I saw *The Missouri Breaks* one time. This horse-thief fella says, 'The closer you get to Canada, the more things

there are that want to eat your horse.' You folks got polar bears
prowlin' all over?"

"Grizzlies. If they came in to the city they'd have to fill out seventeen different forms in two languages, requesting permission to
eat those horses. That fellow in the movie wouldn't need to worry."

"Turn here. Left. This place ain't nowhere yet. Now we're off
to somewhere."

On their left they passed what he took to be a cotton gin – a
large barnlike building with walls and roofs of rust-stained corru-
gated iron, snatches of white fluff caught against corners and
hanging in shreds from trees. Across the road, an elderly gentleman with a wide pink face yanked the peak of his baseball cap at
them from his chair on the front porch of his shack. "Poor ol'
John Quincy Smith," she said. "Used to work at the mill. Got
laid off. Doctor says he's got something growing in his head,
wants to go in and operate, but ol' John Quincy says he don't
want nobody takin' off his head. He's going to sit there waving
to traffic till he dies."

The road dipped and swelled up to hump over a nearly bald
hill, then curved and curved back again to go flat out across a
swamp of snags. Though she said nothing, he was aware of the
heat of her beside him. There was something vaguely disturbing
in his awareness of the two brown legs pressed tightly side to side
in his car – her skirt was hiked up to just above her knees. A man
could go right through life and never know for certain what it felt
like to run his hand down a leg like that. It made you aware there
were textures you might never come closer to in all your life than
just imagining.

"Now slow," she said. "Now slow *down*." A cow looked up from
behind a fence. "Now turn. This is my gate."

Galleries   *97*

He turned onto the dusty driveway and stopped. Above them, children went flying across a yard to throw themselves down on the steps of a long gallery where adults sat looking. Tin roof sagged. Chairs and machine parts and piles of lumber and a shiny white washer sat under the sloping brow of the roof, part of the crowd. "How you like this?" she said. "Get that camera. You go'n' meet my whole damn family and every single one's just crazy about gettin' their picture took!" She was out of the car and already waving an arm. Faces split open into grins. Arms pointed. One huge belly shuddered. Two small children and a dog came rushing downhill, stirring up dust. "Don't you get that candy on this dress! Here – you crazy dog! Go lick this fellow's face, he needs it more than me."

"A government big-shot man from up north," was how she introduced him to the crowd. Heads nodded, muttered, made not-unfriendly faces at him, though nobody offered a hand or invited him to sit. All chairs were filled; chickens had one to themselves. A long-legged man with the hooded eyes of a lizard looked him over, then went inside, shutting the door behind him. The others seemed to be waiting for this young woman to spring something on them, as if she, not he, were the one to be watched. Send a daughter off to college and you don't know who she's going to bring home next. A round-faced youth nodded a solemn greeting, and put two small engine pieces into the basin of gasoline between his feet. An old man with a face the colour of dry ashes slept on, his head on a sack of spilling rags, his fist opening and closing like a baby's against his forehead.

She addressed them from out in the yard. "This man takin' our picture to show everybody back up there in his gov'ment. Now you just hold it, and smile."

A heavy woman hauled on the sleeping man's arm, but the waitress told her to stop. "He sleeps all day in his life, let him sleep in the picture. We goin' open up a magazine one day and see ourselves spread out wide, with ol' Sam a'snoozin' away in front of the eyes of the world." Everyone laughed. "How we doin'? This what you want?"

Yes, he supposed it was what he wanted. It was too precisely what he'd wanted. This young woman with the burnt-almond skin had all but manufactured it for him, like a tour guide lining up a busload of Japanese tourists on the steps of the Legislature.

Before he could take even one picture, he had a sudden glimpse of what would happen next, and was immediately aware that he'd started to sweat. He saw her laughing when he turned to go, he saw her holding him back; "C'mon, you ain't photographed all Miss'ippi yet!" He saw her lead him over the grassy hill behind the cabin and down into pasture and scrubby brush. "Here your picture, son," she would say when they were well down into the pinewoods. "How your Momma goin' like this?" She would turn, flash her teeth, and undo buttons down the front of her dress. "This what you want to take home from Miss'ippi?"

My God. What *did* he want to take home from Mississippi? His hands had begun to tremble. He'd gone weak all over – shame. None of that was actually going to happen, he knew that, but the frightening thing was what it suggested. About him. About the scene he was looking at now: seven, eight, nine people all showing their teeth to a total stranger, bracing themselves to go *pop* right into somebody else's notion of who they were. Even the one who'd gone inside was peeking out the window.

Of course he couldn't take the photo now. "I'd really rather catch them going about their natural business," he said.

The young woman widened her eyes. Several of the people on the gallery laughed. "You think this ain't their natural business? Let me tell you, Grizzly Bear, this is just about all these folks ever do!"

Though they grinned as if they were proud of this, he persisted. "Maybe if we went inside. If your mother, or your sisters, or someone, were making supper."

This time they laughed. "Mister," she said, "nobody here got the energy to fix some supper now. Not until this sun's gone lower in the sky."

He saw them now as actors, arranged in expected postures on their stage. Whatever "real life" they belonged to was something he was never going to see. He could stand here and snap a thousand photographs of this crowd and never capture even a single detail they hadn't intended him to have. When he got around to staring at the prints, there wouldn't be a single surprise swim up out of the patterns to claim his astonishment and declare itself a genuine fact of life. Nothing more than he could find in postcards.

He could not even be sure, now, that these were her family and not just some strangers she'd spied from the road and decided to scare into submission with her "government man." She may have been playing games with him since the moment he'd walked into her restaurant with "tourist" and "Momma's boy" written all over him. How could he know she hadn't put on every word of that damn accent – copying off the TV shows she figured he must have seen, the books she knew his mother had read? Laughing at him the whole while. She was capable of it. They were all capable of it. He was a fool, had let himself be caught out as a fool. He had to get out of here fast.

A picture that wasn't stolen wasn't worth taking. He believed that – why hadn't he stuck to it then? And now he could think of no graceful way out, except to go through the charade of pretending to discover something wrong with the camera. He held it up, aimed through the viewfinder, saw all of them frozen in attitudes of eager co-operation for whoever it was this young woman had brought here and told them to pretend to trust. He pretended to discover that the shutter-release button would not go down. He shook the camera, cursed, apologized. "I'll have to find a shop to repair it." Actor acting for actors.

"Maybe bang it on that rock'll do it some good," she suggested. "Maybe drop it in Zack's gasoline, clean it out."

"I'm sorry," he said. He stuck out his hand, which she regarded as if he were offering her a tip she couldn't see. He tried to make light of the situation, backing toward his car. "Well, at least you got a ride home out of it." But that face would not ease up. "All this, and I don't even know your name."

She followed him down the slope and stood back on a clump of grass while he got in the car. He rolled down the window. "I'm sorry," he said, not even sure why he was apologizing – on the slim chance that she was genuine? For being unable to tell.

For a moment he saw the others waiting too, up on their crowded gallery – all watching. Then, just as he was about to start forward, she said, "Mister, my name ain't all you don't know!"

⁓

That evening they ate in their motel, out on the south edge of town where three different kinds of frog songs came hollering up out of a swamp. His mother had been too absorbed in her work to want to dress up and go out. After she'd soaked up all that special library room had to offer, she'd walked back through the trees to the writer's house and found herself in a conversation with some gentleman who'd been strolling through the grounds. "This was one of those perfect soft-spoken Southern gentlemen. Educated in Virgina, of course. He called me *Ma'am* and told me this and that about the people who lived in the neighbourhood. We watched an old black gardener at work and he said this most amazing thing! He said he didn't mind 'nigras' when they were 'nigras' but he hated them when they thought of themselves as 'blacks.' Imagine saying a thing like that today. You'd think that no time had gone by at all. He was there for the rose garden, he didn't know a thing about Faulkner, and yet I wanted to say, 'Why that man invented you!'" She smiled as she raised her fork to taste the pecan pie. *That man* had apparently invented everything.

"You told this gentleman where you're from – *Shreve's country?*"

It was something she was used to, his half-serious accusation that her interest in Faulkner was partly because one of his characters had come from Alberta. Little more than a name, Shreve was mostly just a pair of Harvard ears to listen to Quentin Compson's droning. Faulkner had never been to Alberta. He'd probably had to look it up in his atlas. A far-off place he was fairly sure that none of his readers had seen.

She brushed his question aside. "Now where was it you went?"

"Out north, into the country."

"His hunting stories! You talk to anyone?"

"Who would I know to talk to?" he said. "Well, I stopped on my way back and talked to this one old man who worked in a cotton gin all his life. He was just sitting there beside the road. I'll bet nobody ever put him into a book."

Her look said: No such person exists.

"John Quincy Smith." The old man had been still sitting out on the front veranda of his shack when he'd pulled the car over onto the gravel by the rust-stained cotton mill. "I thought I'd take a closer look at it," he said. The old man had leaned forward in his cane-bottom chair to shake hands, but fell back right away, as if even that was too much effort for him. Both slippered feet were up on a padded footstool. A walking stick leaned against the wall. Beside him, a cup of dark liquid sat on a large metal spool set on end. Weeds grew up through the cracks between boards. He admitted to having worked in that mill for most of his life, but he'd been laid up now for years, with a bad leg, and was not much good for anything any more but sitting.

"They come running across for advice when they get into trouble?"

The old man smiled shyly and looked to one side. "Nobody needs my advice."

"No family?"

"Nawsuh."

"Neighbours keep an eye out for you, I guess."

A twinkle lit up in the small pale eyes. "Neighbours lookin' at you this minute."

Gordon Bryce looked, but saw only dark reflections of trees in the windows of houses around. No one else seemed to be outside. "I was going to ask you to show me that mill," he said. "It looks empty. I've never seen a cotton gin in my life."

The old man looked as if he doubted that. "Couldn't walk that far. Wouldn't know what to tell you anyhow. A mill's a mill. There it is, go see for yourself."

He had got halfway across the pavement when the man called

out. "Most folks that stops they want to take my picture. He'p
yourself if you like. If that doctor's right you better take it quick."

"So you took his photograph?" his mother said.

"Not even when I saw I could get in a whole row of spread-out
broken chairs and lumber and window screens and glass jugs and
even a toilet seat. And probably people looking through the
windows that I couldn't see with my naked eye."

"The cotton gin, then. I'm not a fool, Gordon."

He shook his head. "When I stopped at the intersection
before turning out onto the road to town, I glanced in my rear-
view mirror and saw neighbours already coming out of their
houses. A white-haired woman in a striped dress. A stooped man
in overalls. A child with a dog. Converging on poor old John
Quincy Smith!"

"Well of course they were!" his mother said. "What did you
think? That's exactly what I would have expected them to do."

He ate his T-bone steak and didn't tell her that he thought she
was wrong to assume her reading had told her everything. How
could she know for sure? He imagined all those people – there
were more, he was certain, waiting just out of sight until he had
gone – he imagined them rushing out to have a good laugh with
the person whose turn it was to sit out today and entertain the
tourists. "Where from? Where from?" He heard them gabbling.
And old John Quincy Smith, looking important: "Never seen a
cotton mill in his life, he says!" They'd squeal at that, accuse him
of lying, they'd shake their heads in the direction of his departed
car. All of Mississippi could be laughing behind his back.

But he had not taken a photograph. That would stop them.
When he was back in Edmonton, walking with Dorothy down by

the river or holding her hand in the cinema, he would be the one remembered stranger who'd stepped out of their familiar land-scape blur to affront the expected pattern of their lives. Let them consider that. No landscape ever came alive until it surprised you. He'd been their surprise. He only wished they could have done half so much for him.

THE CROSSING

Sitting just inside the great slanting windows at the front of the observation lounge, Leanne Collins could almost believe this ferry was ploughing through the choppy waves just for her – rushing her toward those steep forested mountains, and all the mainland world. This could be a private run, a special mission. No one else's journey would have such urgency.

Of course she was not alone on the ferry. There could be hundreds, unseen, behind her. A woman who'd been sitting against a side window came over to stand nearby, perhaps to see what had caught Leanne's attention. The highway was a deep scar scraped cleanly along the side of the nearest mountain, suggesting a sort of waistline. Winter sunlight flashed off fleeing vehicles. Below this road, houses clung to the rocky slopes, some of them propped up by posts that looked, from this distance, no more substantial than Popsicle sticks. And off to the right, beyond a series of stubby peninsulas, the crowded and shining white pillars of the city seemed to grow up at the water's edge as if on a tethered raft. The woman sighed. "They'll be opening the big doors any minute now," she said. "Down below."

Leanne knew this already. The two great doors of the car deck would part, and roll inward, opening up a gap large enough for

coachline buses and transport trucks and rows of ordinary cars to drive through. There was a time when foot passengers disembarked down there as well – pressing against the rope until it was removed, then rushing up the ramp ahead of the vehicles, with impatient motorcyclists revving engines at their heels.

This woman was someone Leanne knew, or thought she knew, though the name did not come immediately. A pleasant face, someone seen here and there in her small island town. A little older than herself, perhaps fifty, with deep laugh lines out from her eyes. One of the Sawchuks, she thought. Angela Sawchuk's aunt? All the family had that unruly hair. "They used to leave the doors open right across," the woman said, "but people started disappearing."

There were very few others in the lounge, winter travellers scattered here and there in the rows of thinly padded seats, backpacks and newspapers spread out beside them. Someone had left a newspaper on the front-row seat next to Leanne. "Ambassador Recalled," one headline shouted. Another began, "Prominent City Financier Questioned In –" His crime was lost in the fold.

"One day this fellow went down and got into his car and drove off," the woman said. She could be Angela Sawchuk's mother. She spoke with her eyes on the world they were rushing toward but at the same time moved over closer to Leanne. "This was halfway across the strait. You must have heard about it." She tossed the newspaper onto a nearby seat and sat. "Sank straight to the bottom, of course." She paused, perhaps to allow Leanne time to imagine a car and driver sinking down through fish and seaweed toward the mysterious floor of the sea. "I knew someone else – got on at Departure Bay and didn't get off at the other end. They never found a trace. Just disappeared!"

Leanne was used to people disappearing. In fact, she was very nearly the only person in her family who had *not* disappeared. Of course she wasn't about to tell the woman this. If she'd recognized Leanne Collins she would already know this fact about her. Otherwise, it wasn't any of her business. Not today, anyway.

Her older sister, Rose, went off into the Cascade Mountains of Washington State several years ago in order to rendezvous with a space ship she claimed had been sending her messages. That was the kind of family she came from. No one had ever found a trace of Rose. No one had ever found their father, either, who had waited until his seventieth year to decide he would really rather be a Tahitian fisherman. He pushed off from shore in a stolen sailboat and that was the last of him. A cousin had simply not been there one morning: his bed had been slept in but his slippers and all his clothes still waited beside it. Either he had been atomized in his sleep or he was off and wandering naked in the world.

They were a queer lot. Even her mother was a bit strange, but in quite the opposite way. She appeared in your kitchen when she was least expected or most unwanted and stayed, smoking, talking, until you had to push her out the door.

Because Leanne considered herself the only sane one in the family, she had always expected to be around when she was ninety-five, still picking up after Ron. She had imagined making her exit in some conventional way, with forty grandchildren gathered around her bed. Perhaps they would even applaud, and pin a homemade medal on her chest for sticking it out to the end. But that was a long way down the road yet. She had only just started her forties.

Where had her relatives gone? That was what kept you thinking about them. Rose could be a New York model by now, or a bounty hunter in New Mexico, unless of course her space ship had actually shown up. She might have walked right down the back of that mountain and taken up with a band of terrorists.

Leanne's father had probably drowned, since he knew nothing about the sea, but you simply could not be sure. She found herself imagining him in a grass hut somewhere, a family of little natives playing with his toes. You could make up anything you wanted about any of them, and believe it true, while almost certainly no one ever made up a single thing about Leanne Collins.

She was *here* – that was why. You could see her, you could drive past her sprawling country house of cedar and brick and glass any time you liked, along the river's edge; you could see her husband driving to his architectural firm in town, you could see her boys walking down the gravel shoulder toward the high school every weekday morning.

Sometimes acquaintances, after a long absence, discovered they had to search their memories for her name. Yet these same people might confess to having had this great long vivid dream about Rose, who had just been named ambassador to Peru. "I could tell you exactly what she was wearing. That Rose!"

If Leanne herself had been wearing snakeskin head to toe, they would not have noticed. Well, they might have noticed but afterwards they would not remember. It seemed that only the disappeared could be said to really exist. You had to be *gone*, in fact, before they credited you with a life worth thinking about.

Even her mother was guilty of this. When she dropped in uninvited she would sit smoking one cigarette after another at the kitchen table and talk about Rose's imaginary accomplishments as if Rose had actually sent home proof that she'd lived up to all her ambitions. "I bet that little devil's living with some rich

stockbroker somewhere," her mother would say. "She doesn't
write because she's scared we'll all rush down and try to sponge off
of her."

"Rose doesn't write because she's ashamed," was Ron's response
to that. It was his belief that everything the members of Leanne's
family did was meant to embarrass him in the eyes of the community. He came from a large family that never moved farther than
a few miles from one another and believed he had married into a
tribe of lunatics, though he considered Leanne to be all that they
were not: the salt of the earth. "Rose would probably like to come
home but knows we'd laugh in her face!"

This woman who could be Angela Sawchuk's aunt or mother
hummed to herself in the seat next to Leanne. Of course she
might not be a Sawchuk at all. Leanne could be thinking of
someone else altogether, a clerk in one of the shops.

What if a person refused? What if a person changed her mind
and decided to stay on the ferry? "If closing the doors is their way
of making sure you don't get off before you're supposed to,"
Leanne said, "what if you changed your mind and refused to get
off at all? What if you decided you just wanted to go back home?"

Obviously the woman had never considered this before. She
looked around the lounge, perhaps hoping that someone in a
uniform would have an answer. Finding no one, she attempted an
answer herself. "I suppose if they caught you hiding in the washroom they'd march you off and make you buy a ticket and then let
you on again." Looking rather pleased with herself, she added, "If
anyone was going to change their mind it would be me. The city
scares me half to death. Such terrible things happen." She ges-
tured toward the waiting skyscrapers, half an hour's drive along
the coastline. "Muggings. Drugs. Awful murders." Even so, she

forced herself to go over once a year, she said. "To do my Christmas shopping. I take the local bus straight to the Pacific Centre and plunge into the crowds. I hold my breath till it's over."

"I shopped in August," Leanne said. Was this a competition? "I wrapped everything and hid them on a bedroom closet shelf."

But she had forgotten to turn on the dishwasher this morning, before leaving the house. And had rushed out without making the beds or phoning Ron at work. She had even forgotten to let the dog out. He was in her kitchen now, wondering where he should lift his leg.

A young man in a turtleneck sweater appeared at the far side of the lounge, crushing a paper coffee cup in his hand before tossing it into the waste bin. Then, holding a striped gym bag, he stood at the window to watch the mainland sliding closer. Houses with plenty of glass. Trees clinging to an almost vertical slope. When he leaned forward to look up toward the snowy mountain peaks, the fingers of his left hand played with the hairs below his Adam's apple. He wore a wedding ring.

Perhaps he was one of those men who married young and then went off to have a good time while their wives stayed at home. She had seen him at the Drop-off Zone, saying goodbye to a friend. They'd laughed, recalling moments from a happy weekend together. They could be part of some athletic team a wife would just as soon avoid. Ron, she thought, did not have friends he could laugh with, though she wished that he had. He discussed laminated beams, vaulted ceilings, and leaky condos with fellow architects, and told Leanne that she was the only real friend he needed.

Of course the young man could have been staying with the friend in order to meet with someone his wife did not know about. A young beauty who'd waited after a game to congratulate him, a childhood classmate suddenly reappearing in his life. He glanced at Leanne without betraying any sign of a guilty con-science, or any flicker of interest either, and then sat at the far end of the front row, with his knees wide apart and his two hands shifting his gym bag back and forth. She had seen her son Cody toss a basketball back and forth between his hands like that while he tried to make up his mind which way to throw.

They were coming up to the familiar tiny island, no larger than a city lot. It was Leanne's habit to wait until the ferry was abreast – where she could see the bare rocks and the twisted trees with their exposed roots – before getting ready to disembark. *Disembark* was the term used by the smarmy actor's voice while giving instructions over the public-address system. Bus people were to head downstairs. Then, after a few minutes, vehicle pas-sengers. Foot passengers would *disembark* from the forward lounge. She thought of herself as simply getting off the boat. *Disembark* made her think of other, similar words. Disembowel. Disembody. Disencumber. Disengage.

"You go over often?" the woman asked.

Leanne thought for a moment. How often was *often*? "Once a month," she said. "To get out of the house for a few days."

"My family would never let me get away with that." This was said with considerable pride.

"Oh, mine doesn't mind." A protest from the witness box. And it was true that Cody didn't mind. But Bert had threatened to take off himself if she kept this up. And would not speak to her for several hours when she returned. Ron took advantage of her absence to work late in his study, poring over blueprints. "They're happy enough when my mother drops in and takes over."

Her mother was only too glad to move in and pamper Leanne's husband and children, her own having escaped her influence long ago.

This wasn't one of the Sawchuks. Leanne remembered seeing her behind the counter at Tim Hortons. She was the manager, accustomed to being friendly to strangers. In fact, she was paid to be friendly to people she didn't know. She would see it as an off-duty part of her job to be pleasant to people she recognized as regular customers, even on the B.C. Ferries, to make sure they kept coming back. Leanne had never noticed her name tag, though of course she must wear one at work. In return, all she knew about Leanne Collins was that she was one of those women who dropped in once a week for a coffee and doughnut before starting her grocery shopping down the street.

"Ron hates the city – like you," Leanne said. "I spent part of my childhood in Winnipeg, and find small-town life a little stifling now and then." She was saying this, she realized, to explain herself to someone who wasn't likely to care. "I have a friend over here that I visit."

The woman picked lint from the front of her heavy coat and said, "Monday morning is a funny time to visit friends."

Leanne might have explained that today's was an emergency trip, but did not. Derek would be racing along the Upper Levels Highway now, in his white BMW. Passing everyone. Swooping down the long slope cut into the mountain and across the curved canyon bridge and up the sharp incline toward the sign that warned you if the ferry lineup was congested. She imagined the two deep vertical creases between his eyes: he would make that little car fly if he could.

He drove with only his right hand, kept the other down on the seat between his long narrow thighs. He would stay in the inside lane until he caught up to someone, then he would gear down, switch lanes, roar past, and swerve back to his lane again. Anxious, he would periodically knead the back of his neck, and frown impatiently at the indirect and indifferent mountain road.

"I'll be there," he'd said on the phone. "If I'm not there when you get off, you won't have to wait very long."

"Yes," she'd said. She had not even got around to dressing when he called. The breakfast dishes were still on the table.

"And, Lee – don't talk to anyone about this. Okay?" ·

"I'm buying everyone sweaters this year," the woman said. "I'm tired of putting a lot of thought into my gifts. Racing all over the place to make sure I get exactly the right thing. And they never care about them anyway. I'll get a nice sweater for everyone and catch the first ferry home."

Cody had recently decided he wanted a whole new sound system for Christmas. Bert wanted DVDs and a leather coat. By the time they made their demands she had already done her shopping: books and CDs, floor hockey sticks. All summer she wrote down things she'd overheard them saying they wanted, and bought them in August. Too early, it seemed, this year.

Ron insisted that this practice made no sense. They would now have to buy these new things as well. "I can wait for next year," Cody said. A good boy – she supposed she ought to start thinking of him as a young man. It was almost creepy the way he could guess what it was like to be a parent. Bert, however, said that if he didn't get what he wanted he would apply for a job on a cruise ship.

They were passing the tiny island now – mostly rock, some moss, a straggly tree bent from years of wind. Leanne checked her overnight bag. There was little inside except her makeup and a change of underwear, things she had grabbed on the fly. Curling iron. Nightgown. Her passport. All the cash she could find in the house. The young man in the turtleneck had already left his seat to start ambling toward the exit door to the outer deck. Eventually they would all step onto a little bridge – a modern gang-plank with railings – and for an uneasy moment could look down into that narrow gap you were passing over, of cold oily water far below.

"One weekend a month is better than nothing at all," Derek had once agreed. "So long as we don't do anything stupid to get our names in the papers." At the time this was meant as a joke.

The ferry swept around the headland and entered the little bay. A smaller ferry had just pulled out from the slip. The large doors would certainly be open by now on the car deck – great curved slabs folded in against the side walls – yet there was probably a rope stretched across the enormous open front end of the ferry, to dis-courage the cyclists from standing too close to the edge, and foot passengers with dogs. An employee stood watch, alert for those who might be tempted to tarnish the company's safety record.

Leanne remained sitting while others stood with feet apart, braced for the lurch and the sideways swing when they struck the squealing, creosoted wood.

She had left her dishwasher loaded but not activated. Why did that bother her now? Perhaps because she could guess who would have to turn it on. And who would have to make the beds. The boys would come home after soccer practice and eat the cheese

sandwiches she had hastily slapped together, and would find the
note that suggested they call their grandmother.

"Today?" she'd said to Derek on the phone. "Now?"

"Now! Catch one of those little float planes."

"You know how scared I am of those things."

"Then hurry, hurry. There'll be a ferry at nine. I'll have my
lawyer with me when I pick you up, we can talk in the car." He
spoke to her, she thought, as he must speak to his secretary when
things were not going well.

"Is it really so bad? Is there no way this can be avoided?"

"Can't you *hear* me?" he said.

He'd tried to restrain the sense of urgency in his voice, tried to
maintain at least a hint of his customary kindness. "My wife is
going crazy. Not even my lawyer is sure he wants to believe me. If
they put together the case he thinks they are trying to – my God!
Think! When the treasurer of a company under investigation
dies in suspicious circumstances – well, you can see. I'll be lucky if
they even let me have bail."

She made an effort to imagine his usually amused eyes, his
quizzical brows, but discovered no hint of them in his tone.

"God knows what will be in the papers tonight, after this
morning's sneering innuendoes. There could be anything, they'll
be so glad to have an excuse to spread me across the front page
again. Do you understand?"

He'd said this as if to an inadequate employee, but he hadn't
needed to spell it out. She was his alibi for that certain
weekend. A hotel clerk, she supposed, would be asked to recall
that he had been accompanied by "an unnamed woman, a tall
brunette in her forties."

But that would not be enough. She would be asked to speak to his lawyer, then to the police. She would be in the papers herself, if he had his way. Her pale alarmed face beside his sidelong contempt for the cameras.

And then?

"We can talk about afterwards once we've got this cleared up," he'd said. "Can you imagine how frantic I am?"

The amazing thing was that she was not frantic herself. When she'd put down the phone it was with a feeling that she had merely come to a moment she had known about for a long time. She did not want to believe there was relief in what she felt, and yet this seemed to be one of those situations where there was nothing you could do except go along. The only urgency, at that moment, had been to catch the ferry.

The Tim Horton's woman was already lined up with others waiting on the outer deck. She glanced back at Leanne, who was taking her time to join the others, and rolled her eyes in a manner Leanne assumed was self-mockery – woman anxious to grab an armload of sweaters and run. The young man, on the other hand, seemed unaware of anyone around him. Rehearsing his story, perhaps – a convincing tale of games played, of goals or points won or lost.

From below there came the squealing of metal against wood and the whirr of electric motors lowering the vehicle ramp. When the short passenger bridge had been slid into place across the gap between ferry and the fixed ramp, they hurried forward past a young man in uniform who stood back to observe – to supervise, she supposed. To Leanne he looked as though he wished his job came with a cattle prod.

And it did seem as though they were all rushing in order to avoid something unpleasant. Strangers impatient to shake off strangers. The Tim Hortons woman was already far ahead, racing for the bus and the underground shopping malls, despite her fear. The young man no doubt expected to be met by his wife, and to go home, perhaps to change clothes for an afternoon's work at the office. And Leanne Collins, eyes searching the world ahead for that white BMW, hurried, hurried, rushed along the sloped ramp from the ferry to join Rose and their father and all the others who lived in the world of the disappeared.

PROMISE

Despite the grey striped suit and blue tie, he didn't look much like a school principal; certainly he didn't look like Squeaky Burns, who reminded you of a weasel as he went slithering around the school looking for someone to pounce on. This Mr. Harington was a stout elderly man with a broad forehead and bulging wide-apart eyes. He looked like a serious bull – Elsie-the-Borden-cow's husband, Elmer.

Unexpected visitors were not unusual at our supper table. Relatives thought nothing of dropping in just before a meal. Friends of the family would pretend they hadn't noticed the time, but eventually allowed themselves to be persuaded. The difference this time was that the visitor was somebody only one of us had seen before.

As soon as my father had got home from work my mother slipped the lunch bucket from beneath his arm and put it out of sight, at the same time urging him to hurry up and shave. "Someone's coming to see you!"

My father slid the braces off his shoulders and unbuttoned his plaid flannel shirt, releasing the rich smell of sweat and grease that came home with him from work. He was a donkey puncher, operating a yarder for the logging company in the mountains behind us – invisible now behind this late-November rain.

"You'll never guess who," my mother sang as she checked beneath lids of steaming pots: potatoes, carrots, beans. My father went into the bathroom and started running water. "Here," she said, handing me a clutch of cutlery. Silverware. "You can set the table. Did you wash your hands?"

I was not surprised that someone was coming to see my father. Men my father worked with often dropped in to get a haircut. (The mayonnaise jar on the kitchen counter was for their quarters and four-bit pieces, the "electric clippers fund.") Newcomers who had trouble with English sometimes came by to have official documents explained. Occasionally someone would ask my father to talk to the RCMP, help spring a drunk-driving son from jail. If this small settlement were in another country – if it were a village in Europe, for instance – my father would have been some sort of dignitary, with local peasants coming for advice and assistance. But here he was only a logger like the rest of them – but one who happened to have lived here most of his life and was known to be decent and level-headed and fair.

"The name Harington mean anything?" my mother called out. She started ripping up lettuce. "Use the best china," she told me. "And the goblets. We'll bring up some blackberry wine." Frowning, she watched a grey sedan drive slowly past our gate, its tires hissing on the wet pavement. "Think back," she called. "Twenty-five years. Don't you remember being a boy at school?"

My father came back into the kitchen rubbing a towel over his face and up over his thinning wet hair. "Harington?"

"Your old principal." She dropped wedges of tomato into the salad. "He phoned this afternoon. He lives somewhere Back East now, but he's on the Island and wanted to drop in." She drove two forks down into the salad and stirred it up from the bottom.

My father looked at me and opened his eyes wide, pretending to be alarmed. "Good lord, maybe he found some old test I failed and wants me to repeat Grade Six. How d'you feel about your old man sittin' at the back of your class, answering everything wrong?"

"Don't be silly," my mother said.

"Or maybe somebody told him I was the one poured molasses on his chair and he's coming to give me a taste of the strap. Whaddaya think?" He showed me his large callused palms that no strap on this earth could hurt. Not after all the years of hard work.

"He said he's always had a soft spot for you," my mother said. To me she said, "He expected your father to go to university."

She'd told me often enough that my father could have been anything he'd wanted: "A doctor, a lawyer, an engineer building bridges. But of course being smart doesn't do you much good when your old man drags you out of school at fifteen and sends you to work in the woods."

At twelve I found the doctor-lawyer part hard to believe. My father had those large rough hands, with nails so stubbornly outlined in black that he had to clean them with a wire brush before going out to a dance. Besides, he liked his work, he liked the men he worked with. When he wasn't at work, he was happy taking the tractor apart, or fixing a fence. If he was as smart as she said, why hadn't he found a way to get an education?

Because times were tough then. This was my mother's one resentment in life. Because times had been tough in the 1930s, she'd had to quit school to work in a dairy though she'd hoped to become a nurse; my father had had to work in the woods though he'd hoped to become a mechanical engineer. This was probably why the matter of future careers was so often talked about at the table. We were to get an education, we were to become whatever we wanted to become. Sometimes Gerry wanted to own a department store, sometimes he intended to drive a Greyhound bus. Meg would be a ballerina. For a while I hoped to be an architect, or an ambassador, or an airline pilot, though my real dream was to make movies.

This was something I kept pretty much to myself, since it was about as impractical as planning to take control of some desert sheikdom. Movies arrived on the screen of the Bickle Theatre from some mysterious, foreign universe that had nothing in common with this world of stump ranches, logging trains, and pickup trucks.

In the dining room my mother examined the table – straightened a fork. "Candles!" she said, and pulled out the top drawer of the buffet.

Silver cutlery. Best china. Wine. Candles. She gave me a defiant look. "I'll be darned if I'll have him feeling sorry for us."

Mr. Harington, when he arrived, was obviously pleased to see his former student after all these years. "Eddie! My goodness, you're looking good." He removed his coat, shaking rainwater onto the kitchen floor. This spectacle would have sent my brother Gerry into fits of laughter if he hadn't been staying over at a friend's. We'd be ducking behind our bedroom door to imitate him, silent-laughing until we were nearly sick.

If Mr. Harington thought my father might have done better for himself he didn't show it. He praised everything: the fields outside, the fences, the garden. This was a fine looking little farm, he said. "Obviously someone knows how to look after it." Someone knew how to look after a house too – everything was so bright! He examined the photos on top of the piano. All three children looked healthy and happy, he said, "obviously well cared for." Mr. Harington strode about, admiring everything. "Fine workmanship," he said, running a hand down the door frame. "But of course I'm not surprised." He sniffed the air. "Something smells good. I haven't had a decent meal since I left home."

"Do you think you'd have known him on the street?" my mother said. She'd removed her apron and put it out of sight.

"I might," he said. He looked at my father out of those wide bulging eyes. "You were what when I left? Twelve?" He turned aside and blew his nose into a blue handkerchief, which he then stuffed into his pocket. "Now that I see you I can't remember what I expected."

My father held up his large callused hands. "You never expected mitts like these, I bet. This crooked finger here was nearly tore off in a winch."

I waited for him to mention the ear that had had to be sewn on when a limb fell from a cedar snag, but he was content to let his hands tell the story of his life.

"I bet his hairline was a little lower too," my mother said as she herded everyone toward the dining-room table. "I tell him to stop wearing a hat, but he won't go out of the house without one. He'll be bald by the time he's forty!"

"A crackerjack at arithmetic!" Mr. Harington snapped his fingers, as though he'd just recalled this. "You could add long four-figure columns in your head."

"He still can," I said.

"Just to prove the old donkey puncher's still got a brain," my father said.

Mr. Harington tapped the serving spoon against his plate to dislodge the mashed potatoes. Though my mother probably imagined cracks forming in her grandmother's china, she didn't flinch. "You probably can't believe your father was ever a boy," he said, looking across the table at me. "It probably never entered your head that he was a promising student."

I wasn't really all that surprised. My father could fix broken machines others had abandoned, he trained newcomers in any number of jobs in the woods, he'd created a tidy little farm out of a rocky stump-ridden piece of land. He helped immigrant neighbours become citizens. What puzzled me was that a principal wanted to look him up even though he lived out here in the sticks – not two miles from where he'd grown up – and hadn't become anything the principal had expected.

While we ate, Mr. Harington filled us in on the various places he'd lived since leaving the Island. Small towns in Northern Ontario. He and his wife had lived in Kingston since he'd retired. He missed the classroom, he said. But things weren't what they used to be, he found himself wishing that students were more like those he taught in the beginning. "I remember every face and name from those early days. You used to wear a yellow shirt."

While the adults were drinking their coffee, my mother lowered her voice to suggest I leave the table to do my homework.

"Homework?" Mr. Harington looked as though *homework* were his favourite word. "Are you as good in school as your father was?"

"I'm all right," I said.

"He's better than all right," my mother said.

Mr. Harington nodded. "I suppose you'll be going off to university one day." He might have been a principal again, cross-examining a student in the hallway outside his office. "Have you decided what you'll study?"

"I'm going to be a ballerina," Meg said. She sat forward, and waited for the gasp of astonishment she was used to. Mr. Harington smiled to acknowledge he'd heard but continued to look at me.

"It depends when you ask," my father said. "One month he's going to be a psychiatrist, the next a diplomat at the United Nations."

"Last week he said . . .," my mother began. "Well, why are we acting like you're deaf and dumb? Tell him yourself. He said he'd like a movie camera for Christmas. He thinks we're rich!"

My face burned.

"A movie camera," Mr. Harington said, stroking his moustache with a stubby finger. His nails were thick, but as clean and pink as the flesh of his palms.

"Well." I took a deep breath. "It will never happen, but what I'd *really* like to do is make movies."

"Movies," my father pronounced the word with a low chuckle, as though he thought his old principal might like permission to laugh.

Mr. Harington's eyes had widened a little, but he didn't laugh. He continued stroking his moustache for a moment, then lifted his glass of wine to his lips. "I don't suppose there's many movie-makers come out of this neck of the woods."

"I guess not," my father said. "This isn't Hollywood. Nobody makes the kind of money here that you'd need to get that sort of thing started."

"He can make a film of me dancing," Meg said, sucking on the end of her braid.

"He's had a lantern slide for years," my mother said. "He draws picture shows on the backs of old wallpaper rolls and sells tickets! It keeps the cousins out of mischief when the house is full of company!"

"You can imagine where his allowance goes," my father said. "Gene Autry. Roy Rogers. Every Saturday afternoon off to town! Claudette Colbert trying not to get murdered on a train."

Mr. Harington regarded me for a moment out of his Elmer-the-bull eyes, then turned to my father. "What happened to that little Morgan boy? What's he doing now?"

I felt a little queasy in my stomach, having the movie-making business kicked around at the table. It was only when other people talked about such things that you saw how foolish they were, even though they'd made some sense in your head. What if Li'l Abner had announced a desire to build submarines? I ought to be grateful that this bulge-eyed principal hadn't laughed in my face.

For a while they dredged up names from the past and tried to figure out what had happened to people. My father was able to tell Mr. Harington that Roger Morriseau lived right down the road, that Dougal McGurr had been killed in the woods when a cable broke. Mr. Harington pulled a notebook out of his jacket pocket and wrote down the whereabouts of anyone my father could locate. "Who was that little cross-eyed girl that cried all the time?"

When he'd put the notebook away, Mr. Harington hauled out his handkerchief and blew his nose. Then he looked at me again and said, "I've got an old 16-millimetre camera I don't use any more." He sucked his bottom lip out of sight, then released it. "When I get home, I'll send it."

Heat streamed up my chest with such force that for a moment I was dizzy. He might have said that Elia Kazan was sitting on the back step, waiting to give me a break.

Both of my parents protested, but Mr. Harington held up a hand. "It's only going to waste." He thought a moment, and then looked at my father. "I wish I'd been here to argue with your old man when he took you out of school."

My father laughed. "A good thing you saved your breath. Nobody ever won an argument with him."

I could almost feel that camera in my hand, the cool metal of its casing beginning to warm, its interior mechanism whirring. I was about to tell Mr. Harington about the stories I'd already sketched out, but he spoke first. "Of course the camera's not much good without a projector. I might as well send that too." Again he held up his hand, anticipating protest. "It hasn't been used in years. It may need a touch of oil." To my father he said, "I must've made a thousand home movies, but we never look at them." Then to me again, "You'll need every cent of your allowance just to keep yourself in film, it's an expensive business."

I grinned at my father, whose schoolboy promise had made this possible. He cautioned me in that half-joking voice parents will use before outsiders. "Having a camera don't automatically make you Cecil B. DeMille."

I didn't hear much of what the adults said after that. I'd already decided that my first film would be an adventure epic. There was an alder grove along the riverbank behind Hughie Woodson's place, where swordferns grew so high they gave the place a prehistoric look. Hughie would be an archaeologist leading an expedition into the jungle.

⤔

The next morning, a Saturday, my father seemed intent on getting away from the breakfast table as fast as he could. The tractor's radiator needed flushing.

"How late did he stay?"

"Too late," he said.

"My gosh, it was two o'clock before we got him out the door!" my mother said.

"I'd forgot what a terrible teacher he was," my father said.

"But he enjoyed it," I said.

My father pushed back his chair from the table, though he had not finished eating his bacon and eggs. "He couldn't teach worth a damn. Couldn't keep order, couldn't explain things. He was probably fired. All those places he went? They probably kicked him out."

It seemed a peculiar way to be speaking of someone who had made such a show of his admiration. "I thought he might have been your hero or something," I said.

"Are you crazy?" my father said. "It wasn't me that invited him here."

"Well, I'm sorry," my mother said. "It was just that he said such nice things about you on the phone."

"I guess he did." My father pulled his chair up to the table again and stabbed another mouthful of egg. Then he said, "You didn't want to be in the room with him. He had this habit of snorting up in his nose, right in the middle of sentences. Drove you crazy. He'd blow and blow until a handkerchief was soaked and then he'd lay it out on the steam radiators to dry. There'd be a whole row of his snotty handkerchiefs drying down the length of the room!" He pushed away from the table again and this time went to the bathroom.

"What's the matter with *him?*" I said.

"It might be a good idea not to mention that man for a while," my mother said, grabbing up some dishes and heading for the sink.

"Is that because he thinks being a logger isn't good enough for Dad?"

She turned on the tap. "He never mentioned logging." She ducked and brought up the liquid soap and squirted it. Then she tossed it back in and banged the cupboard door shut. "First, he noticed that jar on the counter and wanted to know what the 'electric clippers fund' is for. When I explained about the men who dropped in, he talked your father into giving him a neck trim. Your dad would never have let him pay for it but of course he didn't offer. He waited until we were settled in the living room to tell us he was trying to make a living selling life insurance." She placed one dish after another into the sink, and looked out the window as she spoke. "We told him right away that we had all the insurance we could afford, but he tried to talk us into it anyway."

I cleared the remaining things from the table and carried them to the counter, hardly conscious of what I was doing, I was so aware of the sense that things were slipping away. "You didn't buy any?"

"He didn't get a penny out of us," my mother proudly sang. "I thought he'd still be begging and pleading when you got up this morning."

My father came out of the bathroom. "He must be in pretty bad shape if he has to come to this neck of the woods for help."

"He was almost in tears before we finally pushed him out the door," my mother said. "He wouldn't take No for an answer. My gosh, I almost started to feel sorry for him."

"He figured it shouldn't be hard to talk an ignorant logger out of a few bucks," my father said. "I ought to phone everybody that went to that school and warn them."

⁓

I decided the adventure epic would be followed by a cowboy drama – horse thieves and gunfights in the stumpy pasture. I thought my dad's old principal might still send the camera to honour a promise. I thought the interest he'd shown in me might have been genuine, even if he thought my father hadn't amounted to much. He might have wanted to help make sure I didn't end up working in the woods as my father had done. For a while I thought my parents might write him, offering to buy some life insurance after all – once they'd realized that for the sake of a little money, they had, like my father's own dad, been willing to sacrifice someone else's future.

I should have known better than that. One evening when Hooker Jackson put his four-bits in the mayonnaise jar he remarked on the fact that the quarters and half-dollars had risen to the top. "Oughta be enough for them electric clippers by now, I guess, maybe won't pinch a fella's neck so bad." I don't know how much money was in the bottle; my father counted it in the privacy of the master bedroom. Afterwards he said, "Let's just say there's enough for the clippers. If you want to come in to town while I buy them, maybe we'll stop at the bank – see if the savings account can afford a down payment on that camera you're pining for. If that old fraud ever has the nerve to come back we'll let *him* make up the rest."

Of course I knew by then that we'd never see Mr. Harington again. But if his broken promise had inspired my father to help me start buying what I couldn't yet buy myself, I was not about to argue. If my father was doing this to prove something to himself as well as to Mr. Harington *in absentia*, that was fine with me. A man who could add four columns of figures in his head was bound to have several reasons for everything he did.

INHERITANCE

I

The telephone call came the day after their fiftieth wedding anniversary while their heads were still humming with the good wishes of relatives, friends, and neighbours. Frieda thought at first that this unexpected gift was just another of the world's rewards. In times of excitement, she was easily confused.

It seemed that people didn't bother to explain things any more. At first she'd thought the lawyer was telephoning to tell her that Uncle Hugh had died. Then she realized that Uncle Hugh was in the room with the lawyer, and the lawyer was calling, at his request, to ask her to be his executor. If he was making his will he must be still alive.

"This *is* Frieda Macken I'm speaking to?" the lawyer said.

"Well yes! Of course it is," she said. She laughed. Sunlight gleamed off the kitchen linoleum. She could see her own cloud of white hair in the polished kettle. "Uncle Hugh is really my husband's uncle. He was my father's best friend as well, long ago. He must have told you that."

"Yes," he said. "Can we take it that you agree, then? To be his executrix?"

Executrix! "Well, I suppose I could," she said. Then, in case she hadn't sounded enthusiastic enough: "Of course I will!" Her stained fingertips smelled of Silvo – she'd been cleaning flatware.

When the lawyer put the old man on the line, he could only say, "Frieda? Frieda?" She could hear he was crying. He was ninety-two years old, he was alone – a lifelong bachelor – and there were no cousins or nieces or any other members of the family living in Ottawa. There never had been. He'd gone there on his own; stubborn old man. Everyone else was spread across the country, most of them out here on the Coast. "Will you come and visit?" he asked, once he'd got control of himself. "I'll pay the fare. I want to show you what you'll get. I'm leaving it all to you."

She could just imagine what she would get, a bachelor's smelly old things – sagging chesterfield and dirty curtains. A lot of junk to throw out. Rags.

"I'm signing the papers today," he said. "I'm making you my heir."

"Oh my gosh!" she said. *Executrix, heir.* It took a moment to remember there was a difference. "Aren't there others you should think about?"

Of course she went out into the burnished fall sunshine and followed the lane past the garage and the rough board walls of the barn and along the edge of the swampy pasture where mallard ducks paddled amongst the reeds, and eventually entered the chilled and shadowy woods where Eddie was oiling his chainsaw, preparing to take the limbs off a jack pine he'd felled. Clearing one more acre at his own steady pace and replanting it with fir seedlings the size of his middle finger. Opening up a view of Mount Washington too, though it was not so wide or clear as the view from her kitchen window, where she could see across the

tops of the woods and up the side of Constitution Hill to the blue
scarred face of Washington with snow on his nose.

Since she'd started having trouble with her feet she was careful
where she walked, afraid of catching a toe on a surface root
hiding beneath the bed of rust-coloured needles. Being careful
meant she hunched over even more than usual; she knew this,
she was starting to develop a hump in her back like an old round
broody white-headed bird.

Eddie looked up. She could see him thinking, *What now?* Once
she'd told him about the telephone call, he pushed back his
striped engineer cap to get a good look at her. "You sure you heard
right? People our age aren't asked to be executors. The ol' bugger
could outlive us both!" He took off his right-hand glove so that
he could haul out a handkerchief from his pocket and wipe the
sweat from his forehead. "What'd you tell him?"

"What could I say? Just hearing his voice made me think of my
dad."

She watched Eddie squirt oil from a bottle onto the metal
teeth, move the chain along, and squirt again. He bit his bottom
lip when he concentrated on what he was doing. "Better watch
out," he said, a hint of teasing in his voice. "He could be planning to move in with us. He'll have you waiting on him hand
and foot."

"Not with this back! I couldn't!"

"I'll take the boots to him if he tries."

Frieda laughed. "That'll look good." She rested her back
against the warm engine cover of his old grey Ferguson tractor.
"Chasing a ninety-year-old man off the place."

Soil was gravelly here, yet Oregon grape and huckleberry still
flourished, and long grass around the base of the rotting older

stumps. He would cut the smaller trees into firewood length and stack them in neat rows, smelling of pitch. Then he would haul the larger trees over to the little sawmill he'd built himself and saw them up into lumber. She slipped a finger behind her glasses to brush an irritation from one eye.

"I'm an old man myself!" He chuckled deep in his throat, as though this were still the ridiculous exaggeration it had been when he'd started saying it a dozen years ago. And it was, in a way. At seventy-six he was still stronger than men half his age. Unlike her – shorter and broader now than she'd been for most of her life, and stooped as well – he was as tall as ever, and slim. "Just let him start giving orders and out he goes on his ear." He placed his foot on the trunk of the felled tree, whose pale bark was spotted with leaking blisters of pitch, and rested the chainsaw across his raised knee. "Stand back, I'm startin' 'er up."

Halfway back to the house, she realized that she hadn't told him everything. She'd tried to get into the habit of writing things down, but hadn't remembered this time. When she went back she had to wait until he'd noticed her and raised his saw, letting the motor idle. "What now?" Then, again he turned it off.

"He's making me his heir."

Again he pushed back the beak of his cap to frown at her. His eyebrows needed trimming again – they grew horns when she forgot to do this for him. "What about all the others?"

"I've been writing to him since I was a little girl. He said none of the others even sent a Christmas card."

His eyes were not convinced.

"Well, can't you just imagine the fortune I'll inherit?" She laughed. "Drawers full of old letters. Tarnished cutlery. Smelly underwear. Who could be jealous of that? Piles of magazines."

"The ol' fool could own a gold mine, you don't know. You could end up rich when you're too old to spend it."

"I'd find ways." She raised her chin in the direction of the grey cat that watched him from the top of a fence post. It had appeared from nowhere one day, weak and ill, and Eddie had fed it. Now it lived in the barn but followed its saviour wherever he went, so long as he stayed on the farm. "I might just find myself a man that knows what it means to retire. Somebody with a nice little house in town."

"I wouldn't put it past you," he said, and stuck out his grinning mug as though to rub his whiskers in her face.

They hung on here while everybody else they knew had moved to town. She knew he hated it when she complained about this. They hadn't all moved to town, he would say, most of them had died! Of course he was right, she knew this as soon as he reminded her, but it was something that didn't seem to sink in for very long.

"Also," she said, "he wants us to fly back and see him."

He laughed, and raised his saw, ready to pull the starter cord again. "Well, I wouldn't buy my ticket till I saw the paperwork, he could change his mind a dozen times before he croaks."

It had got so she would find herself going out to interrupt him three or four times in a morning; it was getting so she'd rather he never left the house. She tried to read, but it was hard to concentrate with this slight blur from the cataract that wasn't quite "ripe" enough yet to remove. Alone, she would get to thinking, wondering how much longer he intended to stay out there, making that racket.

She knew he would stick it out as long as he could. After a lifetime in the bush he wasn't about to sit around in his armchair, he'd made that clear enough. He'd worked for forty years in the logging camp while he made improvements to this little stump ranch evenings and weekends. Now that he was home full-time, he saw no reason to stop. Each morning he filled the fuel tank on the chainsaw and worked out in the back acres until it sputtered out. After lunch, he'd go outside again and start up the little sawmill he'd built from salvaged parts, cutting his trees into lumber he would then give away to his brothers, or to friends, to build sheds for their machinery and horses. He seemed to think that everyone else retired to a rocking chair and sat waiting to die of boredom.

Well, today he was going to be interrupted whether he liked it or not. Reg and Kitty, Buddy and Grace. Also the boys and their families, once they'd checked out of their motels. Meg and Carl and their girls. Dropping in to talk about last night's Golden Anniversary party. He could hardly go on working as though they didn't exist, though he'd probably like to. The others couldn't find enough to do, was what he said about them. They wanted to *talk*. "Nobody around here's ever satisfied just to have a good time, they have to talk about it afterwards."

As she came up past the fenced garden, a black sedan on the highway honked repeatedly as it sped along the length of the field and past the house. She waved, though she didn't recognize the car. She didn't know one car from another any more, they all looked pretty much the same.

Since the road had been widened, the traffic raced across what had once been part of their front lawn. Close enough to see faces if they ever slowed down. "Seventy acres and you parked your house practically on the centre line!" said people who hadn't known them long. "How do you sleep at night?"

Of course the highway hadn't always been this busy. But Eddie had to make a joke of it, acting as though it were all her fault. "Frieda always wanted to live in town, with the street right under her nose."

Before they'd built the house he'd drawn a picture of how he wanted it to look on the outside, which was how he would mostly see it – a rectangular stucco box with a red shingle roof. It had been her job to decide where the rooms should go, since she would spend her time inside them. She'd hammered, sawn, held studs in place, worked as hard as he did, right beside him.

That was forty years ago. There had been the three children then, to fill up those rooms with their noise. Now she kept the local radio station on, turned low. Birthday messages for someone's Uncle Jim on Cortes Island. A white kitten lost on the Lower Road. Garth Brooks with his latest hit. She didn't pay much attention, but sometimes the words of a song would distract her long enough to make her forget how much baking powder she'd put in the bowl. She'd been famous once for her baking, but lately she'd needed a variety of ways to disguise a flop. Some things could not be saved, even with whipped cream, fresh berries, or a custard. She kept a slop bucket inside the basement door for Eddie to toss to the chickens.

It was another beautiful British Columbia morning today, the announcer said. He said this every morning, whatever the weather was like. He said it even when the rain was pouring down on them like a cow, as Eddie put it, pissing on a rock.

II

Last night's party had been held in the Community Hall, a
hundred metres down the highway – rent-free for anyone who'd
helped build it. Eddie had worked on much of the volunteer con-
struction during weekends for most of a year. From the outside it
could have been someone's barn: unpainted cedar shakes, hip
roof, a row of tall narrow windows. A baseball diamond had been
cut into the woods behind it. Inside, plain green plywood panels
covered walls and ceiling, nothing fancy. This was not a palace,
but it was built to last.

When Eddie and Frieda arrived, most of the men were out in
the evening sunlight, leaning on cars, putting off going in. She
saw Eddie's brother Reg slam his truck door and come puffing
across the gravel, his high-heeled cowboy boots stabbing quick
tiny steps, his cupped hands paddling beside him. He pounded up
the steps to stand beside Eddie, then bent over to catch his
breath – groom and fat best man by the open door. Reg's mouth
fell open in a loose round O, making his wide pink face more
than ever like a giant baby's. Even when he was wearing his best
suit, as he was now, that cowboy hat never left his head. He still
smelled of the horses he no longer owned.

Eddie was in his dress suit too, which made him look especially
tall and slim beside his brother. He'd refused to button the jacket,
though, and still hadn't pushed the knot of his new red tie right
up to the throat. He felt strangled in a tie but would not have
come without one.

"Your boys here yet?" Reg said.

Frieda indicated where Rusty was talking with a friend on the far side of the parking lot. His wife and children were somewhere in the crowd. "Gerry may be still on his way."

Gerry had wished them a Happy Anniversary on his mainland radio program this morning at breakfast. He'd phoned to tell them to abandon their local station for a change and listen to his. Then he'd played "Silver Threads Among the Gold" and invited his parents to call him on his phone-in show. Frieda and Eddie had argued so long over who was going to do it that Gerry had phoned them and insisted they talk, one after the other, about the secret of a long and happy marriage. They didn't have any secret, they admitted, feeling silly. Complete strangers on the mainland phoned in to congratulate them.

Of course they hadn't expected Meg to be here. Because her concert commitments in Europe were always made a year in advance, she and Carl would usually not arrive for their annual visit until the children were out of school for the summer. But she had surprised them, she'd shown up last night, with her family, and was somewhere inside now, lost in this noisy crowd.

There must have been nearly a hundred people seated at the tables down the length of the hall, all of them clapping and whistling as Reg and Frieda's sister Lenora led them to the head table and instructed them to sit behind the tall wedding cake. Reg sat to one side of them and Lenora to the other, just as they'd done fifty years before. The air smelled of fresh-perked coffee and almond icing.

Naturally, Reg and Kitty got out their guitars and sang before anything else was allowed to happen. After years of dreaming about a visit to Nashville, they'd finally gone last summer in their motor home. All of them had gone – Reg and Kitty, Buddy and

Grace, Eddie and Frieda, Martin and Edna – this family travelled in packs. Reg and Kitty hadn't been allowed on the stage of the Grand Ole Opry, of course, but they'd come home acting as though they'd been transformed into stars. The same old songs they'd been singing for years were given an extra boost: "I Fall to Pieces," "In the Blue Canadian Rockies," every chance they got. Today they sang "Bluebird on My Windowsill," for old-time's sake, and yodelled a duet.

Because Eddie hated country music, Frieda put a hand on his thigh to caution him against showing it. Nobody ever thought to ask him what he liked. Nobody would have guessed Peggy Lee.

When Shorty Madill stood up to make a speech she knew it was going to be a long evening.

"The thing about Eddie is," said Shorty, who'd worked in the woods with Eddie most of his life, despite a bad break to his leg from a broken guy-wire, "all you gotta do is look at how he's treated that little stump ranch and you know he's someone you want on every committee." He set his legs wide apart, as though bracing against an attack. "When he retired, Frieda here, she said maybe now they could move into town like Reg and Kitty and live in luxury, but Eddie says, 'What'm I gonna do in town? I gotta be clearin' land.' Clearin' land is what he's done all his life, tidying up the messy world for man and beast, making the place a little better for us all."

Eddie put his fingers in his mouth and gave the quittin'-time whistle.

Shorty didn't quit. "The only trouble working with Eddie is he's so damn honest he could drive you crazy. You ever try to bend the rules when he's around? Oh, he don't make you feel like a crook or anything, he just shakes his head a little sad, like this, and says, 'Seems there oughta be a better way than that.' He'd sell his grandchildren before he'd tell a lie."

Everyone laughed. All of this was true. Eddie muttered, "I'll wring the sonofabitch's neck."

"And how's about our Frieda? Half a dozen fellows in this hall knew what kind of wife she'd be and thought they'd try their luck. But she had eyes for no one but Eddie since she was a little girl! In tough times Frieda's at your door with a loaf of her homemade bread, rolling up her sleeves and digging *in* – whatever needs doing. She got into the habit of helping people and just never stopped."

"Oh my gosh I'm gonna be sick!" Frieda flung her arms out wide and made as though to throw herself off the side of her chair. "If I was that perfect I woulda died of boredom long ago!" She raised her voice so everyone could hear. "What about the time we got run out of that Kamloops campground? Who's gonna tell about the time we got kicked outta Reno? That won't get anyone into heaven."

Kitty jumped to her feet. "Shorty, shut up and sit." Tiny Kitty Macken stepped up in her white cowgirl boots and stood on a chair. She'd traded in her leather fringes long ago for cotton granny dresses, but she still wore too much makeup, dyed her hair as black as soot, and heaped it high with curls in the manner of old-time country singers. "Fourteenth floor of this big hotel and complaints came up from the *first*! It was Frieda made the most noise. Eddie was almost as bad."

"Well, Indian wrestling gets loud!" Frieda said.

Kitty shushed her. "We were all down to Reno for New Year's. The usual bunch. Drove down in our RVs but stayed in that fancy hotel for just one night, a treat – all of us side by side down the fourteenth floor. Our bowling tournament down the hallway brought up the first complaint. We don't know if it was our hollering that did it, or the rye bottles clanging inside the wastepaper baskets. People on the first floor couldn't hear themselves think. That's what their little yellow note said – Grace here grabbed it and swallowed."

"It was Ladies Wrestling got us booted out," Grace shouted from one of the tables.

"Frieda was down on the floor," Kitty said. "Come on and show them."

"Now?" Frieda said. She stood up, smoothing her dress down over her hips. This was a new dress, bought for the occasion – avocado green, with a lace overskirt and a bolero jacket. She'd had to lose ten pounds to fit into it – two months of cottage cheese and fruit.

"What're you doin'?" Eddie said, taking hold of her elbow.

But Frieda shook free. What was a bad back when there was an audience?

In front of the head table, Frieda straightened her shoulders the best she could and assumed the stance of a bossy queen. "I'm not laying on that floor!" With chin out, and one finger pointing down, she commanded, "Somebody throw down their coat!"

Buddy Macken hollered "Wait!" and knocked over his chair in his hurry to stand up. He and two other men dragged one and then another bench over from against the wall, and went back for a third. Reg rushed to the storage room and came out carrying a roll of the paper used for covering the tables, which he unrolled down the length of the side-to-side benches. Then Buddy offered Frieda his arm, and helped her to sit, and to lie back, and then lifted her feet to rest daintily at the end of the triple-wide bench.

All of this was done with exaggerated gestures, all of them behaving as though they were performers in a circus, setting up the next eye-popping act.

People stood up to see this. Someone whistled. "Frieda's still a sport!"

Eddie growled, "You won't have to listen to her moaning later!"

"Who says I won't?" the same voice shouted back – Paul DeSoto. DeSoto had never had a chance with Frieda, he'd had to make do with poor Dora McIntosh, who was already in a Home.

"Where's Grace?" Frieda said to the ceiling. She folded her arms across her chest. "It was Gracie that was down on the floor beside me, don't forget."

Stout Grace hurried across the dance floor, pumping her short fat arms. "That paper better not be dirty, I paid to spot-clean these slacks." Her eyes swam out as big as two bright trout behind her fishbowl glasses. She sat and brought up her legs and flopped back so that she was lying next to Frieda. Head to foot. Hip to hip. Her wide overblouse was a gaudy jungle of exotic flowers.

"Now remember," Kitty said to the crowd. "This was right in front of the elevator doors."

"And both these lovely ladies were wearing big corsages for New Year's," said Reg.

"And pointed hats on their heads," Kitty said.

"And everybody around us placing bets!" Grace shouted up.

"I'd bet on Frieda right now," called Shorty Madill. "She's still got sexy legs!"

Kitty stomped one of her tiny white boots. "I'm tellin' this!" She waited until there was quiet. "So Frieda and Grace're down on their backs like this, and lifting their nearer legs as we counted down. *One! Two!*" Frieda started to lift one leg. "Don't do it in your dress, you'll get us in trouble again!" Frieda dropped her foot so hard she hurt her heel, but Grace stuck her leg up as high as she was able, until her cuffs fell back to show her thick calf and rolled-down top of her nylon. "And just as we holler *Three!* and the legs come up, the elevator door slides open and there's this fellow in a suit and a little tag on his lapel – the manager! Itty-bitty moustache twitching! He just stood inside the elevator staring at the bunch of us lookin' back at him until the door slid closed across his face. We waited for it to open again but it didn't. The son-of-a-gun went down to his office and sent up his security police to hustle us out. Everybody had to pack up and move to the RV park! I bet that manager's talkin' about us yet!"

Once Frieda had been helped to her feet, she hugged Kitty – best friend since school days, when they'd argued about who'd get Eddie Macken and who would have to settle for Reg. Then she hugged Grace – good friend since the day Ned hired her as housekeeper, years before they married. When she'd returned to her seat behind the wedding cake, she took out her compact and looked into the mirror. Her glasses had been knocked a little crooked.

Eddie said, "That little show'll look good on the society page. The chiropractor will think he pulled off a miracle."

"Maybe he did."

"That mean no groanin' tonight?"

"That means I'm not ready for the Old Folks Home just yet!"

Eddie laughed. "Don't worry. Once they get wind of your carry-on, they'll refuse to take us! When we're living in cardboard boxes under some bridge you'll have no one to blame but yourself."

III

Frieda stood in the aisle to get some of the kinks out. You could sit only so long on a plane, her ankles were already swollen. "I can't believe we're travelling alone. I keep wanting to turn around and holler something to Kitty. Imagine what Grace'd say about that lady's hair."

She didn't want to admit that she felt a little anxious. More than a little anxious, in fact, which may be why it had taken them four months to get around to going. They weren't used to lawyers. They weren't used to travelling to cities alone. What they were used to was taking everyone with them.

"I hope he's not senile!" she said. She caught the eye of a man at the window on the far side, a middle-aged man in a yellow jogging suit. "He's always been a little funny in the head – you're the first to remind me of that." The man at the window nodded. She smiled.

Eddie tugged at the back of her white cardigan, where it had got hiked up across her shoulder blades. "Your petticoat's showing." He glanced up and down the aisle in case others had noticed.

She laughed as she shook out the skirt of her dress. They were so used to travelling in a pack their conversations seemed meant for an audience. "Off to collect our fortune!" she said, for those who might overhear. Then she fell silent, pensive. There would be a house. Even a small house was worth something. She did not like herself for thinking this, but it wasn't as though she'd planned it. The money from a house could make a difference. Of course, he might have to sell it himself in order to afford a nursing home, and then go on to live another twenty years.

I hope he does, she told herself, and snapped off other thoughts. "I finally told the others," she said. She turned out the collar of his yellow shirt where it had got folded in somehow against his neck. A rough, weathered, outdoor neck. She imagined all the other men on the plane were in business, with pale protected skin. "Well, I told Kitty, and she's bound to tell it around." The woman behind Eddie would naturally wonder who Kitty was. "Since she's the sister-in-law who likes to gossip the most."

He shook out the pages of the *Vancouver Sun* and folded them back. "So what did she say?"

"Surprised. She didn't even know I'd been writing to him. She said she'd never guessed I was such a cold-blooded little schemer when I was small." Frieda laughed, because of course Kitty hadn't meant it. The woman in the seat behind Eddie looked up and smiled at Frieda – sympathy. She was about Frieda's age, a little too large to be wearing bright pink. Frieda smiled back. "She said Uncle Hugh had probably squirrelled away a fortune, we could get ourselves a villa on the Riviera, or buy the Grand Ole Opry outright – make and break careers!" The woman looked down again, discreetly, and concentrated on the book in her lap. Frieda tilted her head, but could not read the title at the top of the page, to know if they had something in common.

Eddie lowered his voice to a sort of rumble. "For all we know, he could be planning to live it up and leave us all his debts."

"Oh *you!*" Frieda said this loud enough for several heads to come up, briefly. But the woman did not look up from her book. "I been thinking, maybe we could buy ourselves a little house in town, and rent it out –" She raised her voice above his protest grunt. "Just listen – we could rent it out until we need it our-selves." Silence. "I mean when we don't want to drive any more, or the farm has gotten to be too much."

"Whaddaya think we're gonna *do* when we get to this house? Crochet doilies? You might as well nail us up in a box."

Others had turned in their seats to look at the man who had raised his voice at his good-natured wife. "I should've known you'd say that," she said, squeezing past him to get to her window seat. She laughed and, before sitting, spoke to the woman, who'd looked up again from her book. "He'll be clearing land forever, this one. Oldest logger on the planet."

The woman smiled again. Eddie did not. She should never have mentioned the house in town. "Well, if there's not enough for anything big maybe we ought to put it toward a trip – for the whole bunch, I mean. Pay gas and hook-up for everyone's motor homes, down to Arizona for the winter. Then we'd all be sharing it."

"You haven't got your hands on it yet," he said. "This plane could go down in Lake Superior any minute."

෴

When the cab pulled up to the curb, the old man was standing in frozen snow at the foot of his steps. "Oh my gosh, he even *looks* like my dad!" His hair was as white as Daddy's had ever been, Frieda thought. Like her father, he wore a plaid flannel shirt, and loose wool pants. With his jaw dropped open for a great smile, he held his arms out wide, ready to embrace them. He may have been standing like that since she'd phoned from the hotel. He would freeze to death in this cold.

"I'm not sure I want to go through with this," Frieda said. "I'll probably cry!"

"You'll have company," Eddie said. "Old fool is already bawling."

Soon she was embracing the old man, who was small in her arms, somehow laughing even though tears were rushing down his face.

"You came! You came!" One hand patted her back. "Oh, Frieda, you really came."

"Now here, let's get inside before we turn to ice!"

His little house was in a neighbourhood of duplexes – large stucco-and-brick boxes with two identical picture windows in the front wall and a set of stairs up either side. Trees without leaves bordered the street, a crust of white snow frozen to their limbs. Children's sleds leaned against walls. Squat snowmen held out rigid broomstick arms on the little square front lawns.

He did not live in one of these duplexes but in a small brick cottage that might have been built at an earlier time. Bushes that were no more than snarled and knotted tangles of limbs scribbled across much of the front wall. On the little porch, they kicked and stomped their feet to dislodge the snow that had already frozen to their shoes. A pale yellow door in need of paint opened directly into the tiny living room.

She could already hear herself telling it when they got home. "He must've kept everything he ever owned in his life. He'd left a sort of aisle through the middle of it – boxes piled high, chester-field and chairs stacked with newspapers and magazines, card-board boxes on the rug, there was even a box sitting on top of the television set, with an electric frying pan and a pair of slippers on top of *that*! I was scared to breathe, in case I started an avalanche. They wouldn't find our bodies for months."

She was scared to breathe because of the dust as well. Dust coated everything. Dust hung in the air, stirred up by their movements.

In her pleasure at seeing him, she might have forgotten the reason for the visit if he hadn't made such a thing of it himself. He was as excited as any child to drag her through a tour of his possessions. Maybe he'd never given anything away before. He took them from room to room, pointing things out.

"That old clock was my mother's. Eighteen ninety-three."

He dragged her by the hand. A good thing Kitty wasn't here, they wouldn't dare look at one another. Boxes sat on tables; boxes sat on boxes; stacks of magazines and papers seemed ready to fall. A dishwasher sat in the central hallway. Another dishwasher sat in the back bedroom. A row of toasters sat like shiny squat buses parked down the length of the second bed.

So here I am, looking at my great inheritance, she thought. She imagined telling it. He even said – not a trace of joking in his voice – "All this will be yours one day!" and stood back to beam with pride. All what? All she could see was a small dirty house full of tacky junk – cheap bargains, stacks of newspapers, five or six toasters, two dishwashers, two washing machines, two fridges, two of everything! There were even two *blenders* – both of them still in their boxes!

"I see them in them flyers they stick through the door," he said. "I take a fancy to them and then when they arrive I find I've already got one. Or two." He grinned. "I mean to send them back but I forget. I'll have to live another fifty years to use them up!" He winked at Eddie, and laughed. His eyes were without lashes, the rims apparently raw. The flesh over his bony nose was so tight the blood vessels showed; along his jaw a mottled pattern of brown patches met and overlapped.

Eventually it became necessary to move stacks of magazines and newspapers off chairs and onto the floor so they could sit. He put on the kettle for tea. "I'll rustle up some supper for us later."

"Oh-no-you-won't," Frieda said. "We're taking you out." She wasn't going to eat anything cooked here. "You can show us around a little too, if you like. We can go downtown and walk."

"It's minus thirty-six, for crying out loud," Eddie said. "We might change our minds when our ears fall off."

Uncle Hugh said, "I don't wander far – scared I'll forget where I came from and never find my way back." He laughed at this, great noisy gasps of air with his jaw dropped open. Round patches of deep pink had appeared in his cheeks. "I might get it into my head I'm the prime minister, and start making speeches in Parliament. Don't want to give them an excuse to put me away!" This, too, he found funny. He stirred a wooden match around in his pipe, then got up and walked across the room to knock the loose contents into a copper ashtray. He hauled a package of tobacco out of his cardigan pocket and began to fill the bowl of the pipe. He stood with his legs wide apart, a little stooped, con-centrating hard on what he was doing.

"You're alone here?" Frieda said. She meant, Does nobody ever come in and clean up this mess, or cook you a decent meal?

"I've always been alone," he said, sitting again and setting fire to the tobacco in his pipe. He drew in several breaths, to make sure it was alive. "Jake Bowers comes over once a week to do a spot of fiddlin' with me. Mrs. Thorpe stops in to check up on me now and then. To see if I've gone off my rocker yet."

"Mrs. Thorpe?"

"Lady who brings me macaroni and cheese. Buys my groceries when I don't feel up to going out."

"I don't see your fiddle anywhere," Eddie said.

"Course you wouldn't," the old man chuckled. "I'd lose it

myself if I kept it in this room." He hurried into a back room and came out carrying two fiddles. "This is the one I used to play at dances. This other one's an antique."

He handed the antique over to Eddie, then passed a piece of old newspaper after it. "It says in there it's worth $70,000. Two hundred years old. Made in England by this fellow, I can never remember his name." Then he looked at Frieda. "That'll be yours too." How often he must have imagined saying this! He laughed.

"Well, I'm in no hurry for it!" Frieda protested.

"You could outlive us both," Eddie said.

"I could," he said. "Or I could fall down the stairs and break my neck this afternoon!" He seemed to find the prospect amusing.

"Well, don't do it before we've seen the lawyer," Frieda said. She adopted the same tone as his, as though all of this were some great joke they were part of. "We have an appointment at three."

⁓

Once papers had been signed, they walked the length of Sparks Street, looking in windows. Eddie made it clear that he hated the cold, even wearing every stitch he'd brought. "Let's get inside." You didn't hear Eddie asking to go inside very often. Of course they paid little attention to him – they clung to one another. A stranger would never guess that Eddie was the blood relative of the old gentleman on Frieda's arm.

Naturally Frieda wanted to see everything. She felt as though she was being offered the city as a place to settle in. She exclaimed over the merchandise in windows, she admired the stone-fronted buildings and stood back to look up at the glass towers, she stopped and listened with pleased amazement at the sound of French being spoken in the street around them. She took a deep breath and watched the crowds of wrapped-up people hurrying by. None of them looked back. She said "Afternoon!" to more than one woman who sailed on past with her eyes on something far ahead.

Eddie found a parking lot amusing. Cars hung with dirty clots of ice were plugged in to electrical outlets like horses tied to a rail. Tall stakes stood at the ends of the rows, where there were probably painted markings buried beneath the piled-up snow. A woman in furs bent down and shot something out of a squeeze-bottle into the keyhole of her door, then inserted the key. The door came squeaking open. At the corner, steam rose from what looked like an old bread van but was a concession stand of some sort, where young people passed cartons of potato chips smothered in gravy out through a window.

"You wrote you were having a cataract removed," the old man said to Frieda. "You had it yet?"

"No, no. That's – when is it, Eddie?"

She should know when it was. If she thought hard enough. But she liked to make more of things than just question and answer.

"Seventeenth of next month."

"Is it a serious operation?" said Uncle Hugh.

"There's nothing to it these days," Frieda said. "Well, I wasn't bothered when I had the *other* eye done."

"You did not," Eddie said.

"What?" She turned to Eddie, ready to be surprised.

He pushed his grinning face in closer. "I was the one had it done, not you!"

"Oh my gosh, yes!" Frieda laughed and raised a gloved hand to her cheek. "Good heavens! It just seems like I had it done. I've been *through* it!" She studied a mannequin dressed in furs. The film on her right eye made the sharp edges of things just a little indefinite. Irritating when she thought about it. Spiderwebs or cheesecloth blurring the sharp edges of the world. "It seems like I've already been through it, but of course it's still coming up."

In the restaurant, the old man ate with such gusto – elbows out, head down, fork flying – that you'd think he'd never eaten a decent meal before. Maybe he hadn't. Still, he paused occasionally, and wiped the linen serviette across his mouth to talk with an equal energy about her father.

As boys together in Owen Sound they'd been a famous pair of country bumpkins acting up in town, he said. They'd started playing at dances young – "Your father played the accordion, me the fiddle, while old lady Macleod tickled the ivories." – and engaged in friendly rivalry over the prettiest girls. "Neither of us was any great shakes as a lover, let me tell you. Winking and grinning from up on the stage was about as close as we ever got to the girls, most of the time, as they flew by on the dance floor. But once in a while a young lady would make it plain at intermission that she was interested. Course it was always your father they was interested in. Anybody could see a hundred miles away that I was a backward sort of clumsy goof. If a girl ever showed any interest I was sure to open my mouth and say something that put her off."

He reached for one of Frieda's hands, and pressed it between both of his. "It was different when we met your mother, though. I give him a run for his money, I'll tell you that. He didn't get Katie without a fight!"

His dentures clacked and clattered when he talked, slithered when he chewed. If he'd had a wife she'd have had him in for a new set long ago. Frieda supposed it wasn't something she should try to take care of in the few days they'd be here.

∝⟞⟐⟜

"We can forget about the villa on the Riviera," she said in the taxi while heading back to their hotel. There was some pleasure in discovering the joke had been on them. Now that she didn't have to worry any more about guilt, they could safely make fun of the whole business.

But Eddie wasn't so sure. "That violin's worth quite a bit. If the newspaper got it right."

"Two toasters! Two washing machines! Two blenders, for heaven's sake!"

"No one ever accused him of being a genius," Eddie said.

"I was scared to sit down, in case I was lost for good!"

But no one had ever looked so grateful. No one had ever looked so pleased to see them. He'd wept again when they'd taken him back to his house after dinner and prepared to leave. He'd made them promise to come back in time for breakfast. He would make them his famous blueberry pancakes, he'd said, if he could find the griddle. She'd looked in every cupboard but no griddle could be found amongst the crowded utensils. He had two of them somewhere, he'd said. Maybe three. He would stay up all night if that's what it took to find one. If he couldn't, he would use one of his frying pans.

"We could open a second-hand store in the house," she said. "There's enough merchandise to stay in business a year."

"Don't apply for a licence yet," he said. "He's only ninety-two."

"My gosh!" she said. "I think I've fallen in love with the dear old soul."

Later, she turned from one side to the other in bed, unable to sleep. Too hot. Too cold. Light from the street came in through the crack between drapes. Someone had a television on. The traffic noise here was far worse than at home! The hotel was on a busy street near an elevated freeway where the traffic never seemed to let up. *Ka-thunk, ka-thunk, ka-thunk.* Cement road, Eddie explained. The noise was from tires crossing the gaps they left so the spring thaws wouldn't turn it all to rubble.

Hugh's hair was white as salt, like her own. This was something she couldn't put out of her mind. White like her father's beautiful hair. And something in his speech reminded her so much of her father's that she felt an ache in her throat to remember it. Owen Sound. "I mind the time your father and me . . .?"

She dared not cry, she was such a noisy crier that Eddie would think she was being murdered. But it was terrible to have got to this age and still feel this awful ache for your parents. She was seventy-two, for heaven's sake! What had she expected? She had thought – well, it didn't matter what she'd thought, she hadn't expected *this*. When she had been lucky enough to have them both until she was into her sixties.

Eddie's hand flopped around the covers until it found her shoulder. "Okay now," he said. "Don't get yourself worked up."

~

Though they'd shown him the date on the tickets and mentioned the party for Reg's birthday, he could not believe they were going home after three days. When the time came, he started to weep again. Then he suddenly brightened. "You'll not go without a gift. It'll all be yours anyway, but I want you to have something now."

He disappeared into the back bedroom and came out with a toaster in the crook of his arm. Frieda was about to protest, but he stopped, shook his head, and went back. This time he came out with two matching suitcases. Oxblood red. She'd had shoes that colour once. Unnatural. Garish.

"Oh no, Uncle Hugh. We've got our own luggage." These were not only garish, they were cheap. Cardboard slicked up to look like vinyl, so shiny she could see her own protesting face.

"I'll never use them," he said. "I want you to have them."

"But we can't take them. We really can't."

His face fell. "You don't like them?"

"Of course we like them!" Frieda said. In situations like this she tended to overdo it. "They're lovely." She looked at Eddie, who was watching her performance with amusement, but she resisted an impulse to roll her eyes to the side.

"You have to take them." He turned fierce. "I want you to have something of mine, to remind you."

"We don't need something to remind us, Uncle Hugh. I'll keep on writing. You can write back."

"You'll come again?" He might have been a small child fearing abandonment. An orphan, maybe.

She glanced at Eddie, who was looking out the window now, watching for the cab he'd called for.

"We'll try."

The vein-marked flesh of his cheeks shone through a wash of tears.

"Oh my gosh, of course we'll take them," Frieda cried. When his face lit up with pleasure, she thought again of her father, who'd been so easy to please.

"Taxi's here," Eddie said.

"Now, give us a hug," Frieda said. "I'll phone you the minute we're home. We'll be back. And we'll have you out to visit us as well."

She could hardly believe she was saying these things. She could not imagine coming back. She could not imagine arranging for him to come out to visit either. He would have to have someone to travel with. When her back ached at the thought of cramming herself into today's plane, how would she ever face doing it again? Old people should ask only the very young to look after them.

He stood in the window and waved as the taxi pulled away. Frieda said, "Chuck them into the first garbage bin."

Eddie opened the smaller suitcase on his lap. "Empty. I thought he might've filled them."

"With what? Pancake griddles?"

He opened the second suitcase. Empty also. "With money. Shares. Gold."

"We shouldn't even joke about things like that. Poor old soul. My gosh, I almost offered to take him home! But I'd be sorry the minute I said it."

"We could just toss them," Eddie said. They were on one of those cement roadways built in sections. *Ka-thunk, ka-thunk, ka-thunk.*

"Don't be silly," Frieda said. "Someone could see and tell the police. They'd think we were terrorists leaving a bomb. Then how would you feel, when the cops came banging on our door?"

"I suppose one of the grandchildren could use them," Eddie said, "going away to school." They would have to put their own luggage inside these, he said, before they checked in at the airport.

"My God, what a terrible colour," Frieda said. She rapped her knuckles against the larger one. "They look like they're dipped in blood."

IV

They were still sitting over breakfast at the dining-room table when Kitty and Reg drove into the yard. Frieda jumped up and turned the radio volume down so that the phone-in voices could barely be heard. Then she dragged the pair of suitcases out from the guest room and set them on the kitchen table so they'd be the first thing Kitty and Reg would see when they came in the door.

"Where's the doorman?" Kitty hollered. "What's the point in being rich if you don't hire servants? Why isn't anyone parking our car?"

She made a face at the luggage. "You bring him home with you, or planning to leave again?"

"My inheritance!" Frieda cried. "Aren't they lovely?" She brushed fingers down the side of one, as though she believed it a treasure. She could see the vague shapes of herself and Kitty in their shine.

Reg scratched in his thin hair and looked at grinning Eddie, who hadn't got up from the table. Kitty twisted up her face. "My God!" she said. "You hit the jackpot all right."

"He thought he was pushing priceless treasures on us," Eddie said.

"We couldn't hurt the poor old fellow's feelings," Frieda said.

They poured themselves coffee from the gleaming silver pot and sat around the dining-room table where she'd set blue plastic placemats over the lace. Outside, freight trucks roared past on the highway, slapping air against the house.

"Okay," Kitty said. "Tell."

Frieda sipped her coffee. "Well, you know me! By the time we got there, I'd convinced myself he lived in one of those mansions with gardeners and maids and three or four cars in the garage! I'd keep the Jag for shopping."

"The joke was on her," Eddie said. "He's got this little old house that you'd have to scrub with Lysol before you'd want to touch it."

"To imagine the inside," Frieda said, "you have to think of three dozen yard sales gathered together and crammed indoors. The place was dirty besides."

A contrast to Frieda's house. She could see Kitty was thinking this while her eyes did a quick tour of the room. Everything was in its place here, everything was polished. The silver tea set gleamed in the centre of the table. There wasn't a speck of dust on the shining cups and saucers of Grandma Barclay's dinner set, displayed along the top of the window valance. You could even see yourself in the floor. A government homemaker came in to do the housework once a week in a slap-dash sort of way, but Frieda could not just give up a lifetime's habit. A house needed daily attention if it were not to become an embarrassing pig-sty mess.

She used her cardigan sleeve to wipe off a thumb smudge she'd just noticed on the silver coffee pot. "Of course he had to play his fiddle for us," she said.

"How bad was it?" Kitty said.

"Bad enough," Eddie said. "Damn fool was grinning like he thought he could charm birds from the sky. It didn't last long because he couldn't remember more than a bar or two of anything."

"Uh-oh," Kitty said. "Either Queen Mary's rose from her grave or I saw Nora's sour face in Buddy's car, pulling in."

"She couldn't wait a minute longer," Grace called from the doorway while she wiped her feet. Thump, thump, thump. Like a bull preparing to charge. "Scared to death you'd start divvying up the fortune without her."

Nora's face made it clear she smelled something going on that she would disapprove of. She circled the dining-room table until she came to an empty chair. She was tall and thin and straight as a poker at eighty-six, as if the only sister in a family of boys she'd helped to raise had an obligation to be regal. She sat and poured sugar into a spoon and waited for Frieda to put a cup of coffee under it. "My father's youngest brother," she said, stirring it in. "Not much older than me. I remember one visit he made to us, when I was quite young. We got on very well."

"He didn't mention that," Frieda carefully said. "He didn't even seem to remember he had other relatives." Nora had always had to be catered to, often through gritted teeth.

"There's plenty of us still breathing," Nora said. "I'm sure Eddie filled him in." Implying, of course, that Frieda had naturally not.

"He hardly noticed me," Eddie said. "He's in love with Frieda. She reminds him of her mother."

Nora studied Frieda a moment out of a dowager's skeptical eyes. "She doesn't look a bit like her mother."

"He claims her mother was the only girl in his life he ever cared for."

"That's nonsense," Nora said. "I remember Father saying Uncle Hugh carried on for years with some farmer's homely widow down a concession road. They were the talk of Owen Sound."

"Well, I don't imagine he's carrying on with anyone now," Frieda said. "His tomcat days are over."

"Frieda's the image of her father," Nora said. "Anyone with half an eye can see that."

❦

The next morning, when Frieda stopped at the general store to pick up the mail, Kitty was sitting at the little wooden table by the window, thumbing through a *Country Music* magazine before heading up to Campbell River for her singing lesson. Kitty and Reg had run the store themselves for a few years, long ago when they were first married. People had stood around to talk, but no one had thought of giving over space to table and chairs and serving hot drinks, as these newest owners did.

"I bet Nora's home this minute writing a letter," Kitty said. "If there's so much as a hanky to be got for free she'll try."

"We can give her one of the toasters," Frieda said. "There's nearly enough for us all."

Dora Svetich went through her daily routine of pretending she didn't know where the Eddie Macken pigeon hole was, though the alphabet hadn't changed in the past fifty years. When she'd finally handed Frieda the mail – the weekly newspaper and a couple of charity appeals – Frieda poured herself some coffee from the Pyrex pot and took the seat across from Kitty. The table and chairs were painted pink – hippies had taken over the store for a few years, and prettied things up. What they hadn't prettied up they'd left in a mess. After eleven years of owning the place, Dora and Norm were still finding surprises they didn't like. Dried cannabis in the attic, magic mushrooms behind the shelves.

"I don't like myself for making fun of him," Frieda said. "Dear old soul. He reminded me of my dad."

Kitty did not say anything. She studied a photo of Barbara Mandrell. Her white cowgirl boots were tucked back under her chair, "Kitty" written across them in letters painted to look like a lariat. Her glued-on fingernails were an inch long, garnet red. "It seems a strange thing to do – to write letters all your life to someone that nobody else ever thought of." Her false eyelashes were so long and heavy that she had to force her eyes wide open to show her surprise.

"It didn't take me fifteen minutes a year," Frieda cried. "I started when I was little. My father's old friend. He always wrote me back."

"I'm *your* old friend so I'll say this once and not mention it again." She crossed one leg over the other and pointed the cowgirl boot straight out so that she could turn it this way and that, examining it for unwelcome marks. She hauled off the boot and licked a finger to rub fiercely at a dark smudge. Her toenails were garnet red as well. "Of course you always did the right thing. And the poor old man was lonely." She put the boot back on. "*Frieda Macken to the rescue*," was said to the boot. Then she looked up. "Frankly, your halo's becoming a problem for me. I never did anything for anyone else in my life that I didn't have to, so what can I expect? I'm sorry, Frieda, but dammit, it seems to me you've always got more than your share of things." She rolled up the magazine and tapped it inside her palm, as though she were impatient to leave. "There, I've got it off my chest, I won't ever say another word about it in my life."

"You certainly will," Frieda said. For a moment she found it difficult to breathe. "You'll say another word about it now. I can't believe what I just heard."

"My big old mouth goes blabbing on. Forget it." Kitty waved the magazine like a wand, to erase the words that had passed through the air between them. "What has ever happened to me in my life? One dream – the closest I ever got was fourth row in the *audience*. I'm happy about your good fortune, but I have some trouble with it too, is all I'm saying here. It even bugs me that I know you'll share it when you get it. You'll do the right thing even then."

"We should've kept our stupid mouths shut," Frieda said. She pressed her lips together and looked out the window. Em Madill was pulling out from the side road into highway traffic. Someone ought to take away that woman's licence. She never looked. "I thought it would be more fun if we laughed about it. How much difference will it ever make to us?"

"None. That's the galling part. And I suppose it'd only be worse down the road if you didn't tell us now. At least this way we can get used to it."

"We?" Did she have to worry about the others too?

Kitty stood up to go. "Pretend I didn't say a thing. I always think I'll feel better if I say what's bugging me, but I always end up feeling even worse."

❧

Frieda wrote to Uncle Hugh, telling him how much they'd enjoyed the trip, how pleasant it had been to see him after so many years, but she didn't see any point in thanking him for offering to pay the plane fare. He'd remembered that he'd offered, of course, but as they left he'd suggested they send the bill to his lawyer. Then he'd changed his mind. "You can take it out of your inheritance when I kick the bucket."

A second letter was just a note, bringing him up to date on events in the family. Reg had come out to help Eddie replace some fence posts. Grace had won a few dollars in a scratch-and-win lottery. An Easter card arrived from Uncle Hugh, with some scribble on the page facing the commercial message, which was in several languages. He thought about their visit every day, he said, and was already looking forward to their return. They must stay in the house next time, he said; he would clean out the second bedroom. Of course he would be happy to pay for their airfare once again!

Her third note mentioned that Eddie was outside playing with his big toy – his sawmill. A load of lovely-smelling fresh-sawn yellow cedar had just gone out the driveway, heading for someone in town. She had baked a batch of bread, and wished she could give him a loaf. Kitty had sprained an ankle in a fall, but was mending fast. In his response he asked who Kitty was, she'd forgotten to say. He said he would give his eye teeth (if he still had them) to taste her bread when it was fresh from the oven, but Mrs. Thorpe brought him a loaf now and then from a decent bakery in town. "Your father was crazy about fresh bread. I mind the time he made himself sick on it. I wonder if you knew how much you put me in mind of him. I never saw much of him in later years but we kept in touch."

She began another letter ("The garden is up. We're expecting a huge crop of tomatoes this year.") in which she intended to bring up the idea of inviting him out for a visit, but put it aside to prepare snacks for Reg and Kitty and Buddy and Grace, who were about to arrive for an afternoon of bridge. The telephone rang just as they arrived.

Once she'd replaced the receiver to its cradle, she went into their bedroom to sit on the bed for a while. She held her hands to her mouth and concentrated on achieving calm. She could put off thinking about it till later. She wouldn't say a thing with the others here.

But during the game, Eddie noticed something was wrong. "What is it?"

She half-laughed, gave her head a little shake like someone coming out of a daydream. "Well, I'm having trouble believing what I heard. On the phone."

"Who was it?" he said.

"Uncle Hugh's lawyer."

"Is there something wrong?"

"Yes. No." She laughed. She picked up her cards as though she were prepared to go on with the game, then put them down on the lace. "Well, his health is failing, yes. And he's moved into some woman's home. Mrs. Thorpe. Someone who's been keeping an eye on him anyway."

"He mentioned her," Eddie said.

"The lawyer seemed to think there's reason to worry. Uncle Hugh's given the woman the power of attorney – turned all his business over to her. She can sign his cheques, everything."

"Well, if she's going to look after him," Kitty said.

"And God knows I never encouraged him to think he could come here," Frieda said. "I feel terrible that I didn't."

"She's a friend of his," Eddie said. "You don't need to feel bad about that."

"Oh don't I! The lawyer says this woman and her husband keep their house full of old men who don't have any family. He's tried to warn Uncle Hugh off her. She isn't licensed by the government so she's never checked up on. People know this, but nothing's ever done."

"Take her to court," Grace said.

"Wouldn't that look good! Greedy relatives fly in to grab it all." There was a catch in Frieda's throat. "No, we'll just have to hope she takes good care of him. Well, I'll write to tell her she'd *better*!"

"Nora will have a fit," Kitty said. "A relative falling into the hands of a stranger! She thought it was bad enough he'd turned himself over to Frieda – related through only fifty years of marriage."

Eddie continued to frown. The creases in his forehead were pale where his hat protected him from the weather. The rest of his face was weathered a healthy colour, summer and winter both. "That's not all he told you."

"It's just that I can't believe it!" She laughed, or tried to laugh. "I might as well tell you. He said Uncle Hugh came bursting into his office and demanded his will back."

Reg groaned. Buddy said, "Old bachelors!"

"He had to give it to him," Frieda said. "He was going to another lawyer to make another will. Presumably in the woman's favour." There was silence for a moment around the table. Reg studied the cards in his hand. Frieda laughed. "So – a good thing we didn't hire servants yet! There goes our wealthy old age!"

"You sure of this?" Eddie said.

"That's what he said."

"Jesus," Reg said.

"Well damn that woman anyway," said Grace, throwing down her cards. "We were planning to hit you up for a loan – this waterfront house we got our eye on."

"There's more," Frieda said. "There's worse. He thinks we're a couple of thieves!" This came out half wail, half incredulous laugh. She put both hands to her mouth.

"Whaddaya mean?" Eddie said. He sounded fierce, ready to get up immediately and deal with the problem – whatever it was.

"I don't know how to say it! When he came into the lawyer's office he was furious. This Thorpe woman was helping him pack for the move to her house and they couldn't find his suitcases."

"Uh-oh!" Kitty said, ten false fingernails pressed to her forehead.

"He remembered us going off with them. He couldn't remember why. She convinced him – this Mrs. Thorpe – she convinced him that we'd *stolen* them! He thinks we stole his stupid damn ugly red suitcases!"

"We didn't even want the damn things," Eddie said. He was angry now. "You tell him that?"

"You'd have to pay me to take them," Kitty said, without looking up from behind her hands.

"I told him I'd mail them back tomorrow rather than see the poor old fellow upset. But he said it didn't matter, that wasn't the point. The point is, he's slipped too badly now, he believes everything this woman tells him, he's going to another lawyer to change his will."

"If he's crazy it won't count," Kitty said, looking up at last. Pleased with herself.

"He isn't as crazy as that," Frieda said. "He's just sick, and scared, and – let's face it – he believes the woman who's been around to take care of him. Who can blame him? Why shouldn't he think we're crooks? Oh, I feel awful! I don't care about his stupid gee-dee will, but I just can't stand it that he thinks we'd do that! We'll have to go back and explain."

"You want to fly across the country to explain that you didn't steal a couple of nineteen-dollar suitcases?" Eddie said. "You better leave it to his lawyer."

"He isn't his lawyer any more. He's dismissed him." She hated it when her voice became a wail. She sounded like a whiny child in panic. "He thinks we're a pair of crooks."

Maybe it was hearing herself say that out loud again that brought her up short. Frieda and Eddie thieves! She laughed. "A new career for our old age. Bonnie and Clyde!"

"I've got news for you," Kitty said. "You won't make much of a living if you can't think of anything better to steal than el cheapo luggage!"

"A whole new opportunity opens up," Grace said, gazing wide-eyed into space. "Maybe we'll join you. A travelling caravan of motor homes – thieving our way across the landscape."

"We can start with that hotel jerk in Reno," Kitty said. "I'd like to clean out that son of a bitch's safe."

"Frieda and Eddie can front for us, to distract him," Buddy said. "Who wouldn't trust a pair of honest mugs like that? Seventy some-odd years of decency stamped all over them."

"They'll have trouble making the WANTED posters convincing," Kitty said.

"It isn't funny," Frieda said. "I feel terrible about it."

"You're damn right it isn't funny," Grace said, hoisting up her heavy breasts. "Me 'n' Buddy were planning to sponge off you for the rest of our lives, but you've gone and let us down. Now I'll have to learn how to point a pistol and make people lie on the floor."

"Well there you go," Kitty said. "Nobody's all that they seem."

"Don't say that," Frieda cried. "As soon as my head hits the pillow that's all I'll be able to think about."

"It never entered our heads until you brought it up," Kitty said. "You two always make such a to-do out of everything, a person can never be sure what's the truth. How are we supposed to know what really happened?"

"You think we stole those stupid suitcases!"

"For God's sake," Grace said. "If you were gonna steal something from the old fart I'd like to think you'd take his silver at least! Or that old fiddle he's so proud of."

"Anyway," Reg said, "we'll arrange to have a weekly game of bridge in your cell."

"Reg'll write a song about it," Kitty said. "How the Upright Pair turned to a life of crime. We'll get ourselves on that Ole Opry stage yet!"

They were still laughing about it when they went out the door. "Last seen leaving the residence of the famous Macken gang," Reg said. "Guests checked their pockets to make sure their car keys hadn't been lifted."

Frieda's laugh chimed out. "Check your fillings when you brush your teeth. You know how light-fingered I've got." But as soon as she'd closed the door she looked at Eddie and said, "I don't think I can stand it!"

v

She would not get out of bed the next morning. She couldn't. She'd seen pigs drop from a blow of her father's sledgehammer.

She'd seen steers collapse from a bullet from Eddie's gun. A moment of stunned disbelief (she'd gone on laughing, joking, pretending she was all right so long as there was company to observe her), then down, all at once, in a heap.

"*Won't* is one thing," Eddie said. "*Can't* is another." He'd made breakfast, and stood in the bedroom doorway, trying to get her up to eat it. "Do I call the doc to send the ambulance out or not?"

"Don't you dare." She stared fiercely at the wall. Familiar old wallpaper flowers, daisies. "I'm not leaving this house."

"Are you leaving the bed?"

"I might and I might not." She flounced a shoulder at him, and flipped a blanket up over her head.

She got up eventually, just to keep him quiet, and ate the breakfast, and hobbled about with her shoulders slumped forward. Her back was one large ache. After a while she returned to bed and lay there for much of the day.

He poked his head in, but she was waiting for him. "It makes me so mad," she said. She was on her back this time, with the blankets pulled up to her chin. "I should just get up and get on that plane."

"You think I want to push you around in a wheelchair the rest of your life?" He used the telephone in the hallway and came back. "The doc's got time for you Tuesday, we'll see what he's got to say."

"It drives me crazy knowing that woman has him in her clutches."

"What do we care about her?"

"I care because there should be someone protecting him. There should be a relative. Think of my dad. He was never alone, he had all of us looking out for him." She rolled over onto her side again, to address the wallpaper. "What if Daddy had been alone, like Uncle Hugh?"

"The old fool chose to live back there by himself. He already knew the woman, he seemed to like her. It isn't any of our business any more."

"It is my business, and I'm going to get up off this bed and fly back there to sort this out if it kills me. Take those darn suitcases out and hide them in the barn, I can't stand the sight of them. I swear they get bigger every time I look."

༼⚭༽

Her letters to Uncle Hugh were not answered. The lawyer wrote to say that nothing more had transpired between him and his former client, but that he understood Mr. Macken to be permanently resident now in the home of Mr. and Mrs. Thorpe. He had no authority himself to protest the matter. On several occasions, Frieda telephoned the Thorpe house and asked to speak to her uncle. At first the woman seemed unprepared to believe the old man had a niece, and put a series of questions to her that seemed like a cross-examination. The suitcases were never mentioned. Uncle Hugh was not called to the telephone. He would be confused, the woman protested. Well, he was sleeping anyway, and shouldn't be disturbed. He didn't wish to speak to someone named Frieda. Letters from a Frieda had been received at this address and she had read them to Mr. Macken, but he had not shown any interest in answering them.

"Tell her we're flying to Ottawa," Eddie said from his chair in the living room where he was working his way through the latest *National Geographic.*

"Just a minute. What's that?" she shouted. The telephone was on a small desk in the hallway.

"Tell her we're coming to check up on her," Eddie said.

"Yes," Frieda said. "We'll be flying to Ottawa one of these days," she told Mrs. Thorpe. The calendar on the wall above the phone had not been turned to the new month yet, though it must be the fourth or fifth by now.

"Not one of these days," Eddie said. "Next month. And tell her we'll want to visit him."

"What?"

"Visit him."

"What do you mean? Just a minute, Mrs. Thorpe." Frieda held her hand over the mouthpiece and raised her voice. "What are you talking about in there?"

"Just tell her we're going to come knocking on her door expecting to visit old Hugh," Eddie said.

"Well of course we will," Frieda said. "He's my husband's uncle," she told Mrs. Thorpe. "He was my father's closest friend. We have airline reservations for the – what is it, Eddie?

"Tell her the twelfth."

"The twelfth."

⁓✥⁓

But Eddie decided that it would be foolish to sit for five cramped hours in a plane when she was still wincing and groaning in her own house. He even encouraged her to postpone the cataract operation, to cut back on the stress in her life. The world would just have to go on having blurred edges until she was her old self again.

"The idea has been planted," she said when she'd got up for a makeshift supper he'd put together out of leftovers found in the freezer. They sat at the little kitchen table they'd bought when they were first married, though Eddie had since covered the wooden top with a sheet of green Arborite and edged it with a strip of chrome.

"What idea?" Though they'd barked at one another most of their lives, it had always been a sort of mock anger. A bit of an act, in fact, since real anger just never happened between them. But patient Eddie was now beginning to get a bit testy, a little tight around the mouth.

"You know what idea. It has been planted in their heads, thanks to that stupid woman." She looked at her forkful of fried potatoes and put it down. She had no appetite.

The Arborite was stained with rings from coffee mugs. Her kitchen was a disgrace, though the cleaning lady had been in only three days before.

"Planted in whose heads, for chrissake? What are you talking about?"

For a moment of panic she wasn't sure what they were talking about. His question didn't link up with anything else. She had to work her way back, forcing her breathing to stay regular. Accusations of theft, the luggage, Uncle Hugh's will. What she'd meant was ideas had been planted in Kitty's head. And Grace's.

"And Nora's, I suppose," she said.

He growled. "You never gave two hoots before what Nora thinks. You wouldn't've married me if you did."

"Reg, then. Reg has always been a little standoffish with me." She jabbed the potatoes into her mouth and chewed. "He's probably glad to think I might have done it. He wonders what else I've taken that isn't mine. I bet he wonders if I got more than my share of your mother's old things."

He stood up and went into the kitchen to pour boiling water into the teapot. "You've read too many books. People got more to do than worry about things like that."

She put down her fork and brought her hands up to rest her fingers against her temples. "My face burns when I think of all those people who came to our Anniversary! Even if they're only telling it as a joke, it plants some doubt in people's heads. I don't know that I'll ever go out again."

He grinned his mocking grin at her, as he'd once done with the boys when they took themselves too seriously. "You could stand on the main street of town with a sign: 'Yes, I stole my uncle's ugly suitcases' and see how many believe you, how many care."

She refused to make light of this. "That isn't the point. It only takes the smallest thing for people to think the worst. I can't feel the same about Kitty and Grace any more and it breaks my heart. I've always been closer to them than my own sisters."

He poured tea for them both. You think my back's not acting up? I'll be damned if I'm gonna lie down and let them think I quit! I'd rather go out and knock down a half-dozen trees."

◦﹊◦

She went to the kitchen window again. Eddie was still outside, helping Reg choose two-by-fours for a shed he planned to build. The radio announcer was taking phone messages from the more remote communities. A student on Texada Island was looking for a copy of *Huckleberry Finn*, preferably second-hand. A lady on Minstrel Island sent birthday greetings to her sister in Port Alice. Eddie stood with his weight on one foot, as he did to ease his back a little, shaking his head at something Reg was saying while he slid a two-by-four onto the bed of his pickup.

What did she care about the sister in Port Alice? She couldn't stand it any longer. She felt a hollow sense of being left alone in the house while the world went on without her.

Reg straightened when he saw her come down the steps. "Eddie says you think Kitty turned against you?"

She hadn't expected this. Nor would she have guessed that Reg could sound so fierce. "Well, my goodness, I don't know." She tried to laugh, to show she didn't want this to be taken too seriously. "Yes. I guess maybe I do, a little."

Eddie looked away, as though he found something of interest on the far side of the swamp. "Kitty don't always think before she speaks. She lets her jealousy get the better of her."

"Jesus Christ!" Reg's wide fleshy face coloured up as he turned on Eddie. "Jealous about what? The damn will?"

"A little, I think," Eddie said, addressing the toes of his boots.

"Please," Frieda said. "Let's not make an issue of this." Tears had come to her eyes.

But they ignored her. "It's tearing Frieda apart that people might think she engineered it all," Eddie said.

With his fat little baby mouth set tight, Reg dragged the two-by-fours from his truck, one after the other, and tossed them back on the pile. "Well, she's just going to have to put up with that, isn't she?" He spoke as if Frieda weren't there. "If she thinks we're such a rotten lot we'll make sure she don't have to see too much of us." When he'd got into his truck and started the engine, he said, "I'm not so poor I can't buy boards at Central Lumber like everyone else."

Eddie chuckled as he watched the truck turn onto the high-way. "He'll calm down in a while."

Frieda was not so sure. "I don't know that I can stand it. Something's happening to us here that scares me."

❧

She often thought of her father, a gentle, humorous man who loved children, loved them even when they grew to be middle-aged. She thought of him when he'd got old, into his eighties, and began to forget who people were, then began to forget who his own children were, and even began to forget who the woman was who cooked his meals and slept beside him in the bed. He didn't lose a hair from his head. When he began to wander away and forget where he came from, Frieda told Eddie that if she ever got like that she wanted him to take her out behind the barn and shoot her. She told the same to her children. She thought of her father walking down the street, not recognizing anyone he met though he'd known them for years, but friendly to them anyway, just as he'd always been. His shoulders were rounded into a stoop, his dark cardigan hucked up at the back. At the traffic light corner, or sometimes far down the dike road, he would be found by someone who knew he shouldn't be there, and taken home.

She often found herself crying when she remembered this, hardly able to believe how much she missed him. Seventy-two years old and missing her father! Missing both her parents. She just could not get it into her head that they were gone, had been gone for years. She still went to the phone with something she wanted to tell them, but had to bite her lip when she remem-bered. Once your parents were gone, who was there left in the world you could boast to? Who else could be counted on to be pleased? If Mom and Daddy were still around for this business with Uncle Hugh, they'd have been pleased at Frieda's good fortune, they'd have understood why Frieda felt as she did about the things that people were saying behind her back.

⌒

It seemed that they might actually go this time. Frieda was up and about for longer periods, her back bothering her less since she'd started taking some new medication prescribed by Dr. Newsom. She was not looking forward to the long flight, but she would go crazy if she didn't see Uncle Hugh face to face, to get this misunderstanding straightened out. However, when their departure was only a few days off, another telephone call from the Ottawa lawyer changed everything.

"I have been speaking to your uncle's doctor, and have spoken with his Mrs. Thorpe as well. I am afraid I have some sad news. Your uncle passed away yesterday morning, after suffering from a massive stroke."

"Oh dear," Frieda said. "Oh poor Uncle Hugh."

"Who is it?" Eddie said from the television room.

"The lawyer," Frieda said. "I'm sorry, Mr. Uh. I don't know what to say. We were going to leave on Thursday but there wouldn't be any point in that now, of course. I mean, I wouldn't be able to talk to him now. I just wish we had got there sooner."

"What does he want?" Eddie said.

"It's Uncle Hugh. He's had a stroke."

"He was a very old man," the lawyer said. He possessed one of those low comforting voices, like a TV doctor. "And I remember him telling me how much pleasure he got from –"

"Is he all right?" Eddie said.

"What?"

"Hugh. How is he?"

"He's dead, for heaven's sake."

"He telephoned me several times after your visit," the lawyer said. "You brought him a great deal of happiness at a time when it mattered."

"Before that woman got her hooks into him."

"Nothing could have been done about that. That is the way this woman and her husband operate. This business had started long before you arrived, she had already won him over, there was little anyone might do at that point to change the course of things."

"And no one ever takes these people to court?"

"It has been tried," the lawyer said. She imagined him sitting behind his wide, shiny, walnut desk, speaking into a phone he didn't even have to lift. "But it is not very pleasant for the relatives, who can easily be made to look bad when there is a will involved. It only needs to be asked, 'Why did this old man turn to a stranger?' Such people depend upon our reluctance to get into these contests. Especially when the old man has signed papers giving the care-person power of attorney."

"And I don't suppose you had any more contact with him yourself."

"No. And I've heard nothing more of a second will, though there is little doubt that the first one has been destroyed. Our Mrs. Thorpe would make certain of that."

Several weeks later the lawyer telephoned to explain that Mrs. Thorpe had not come forward with the expected new will. "When I called, she reluctantly admitted that there isn't one.

Naturally the original document does not exist any more, since the old man had insisted on being given all the copies to destroy."

"So what will happen now?" Frieda asked.

"Under the circumstances, the estate will be divided evenly amongst all of Mr. Macken's brothers and sisters, with the shares belonging to deceased brothers and sisters going to their surviving children." Although Frieda was no longer the executrix, he said, he had taken steps to appoint her as administrator of these legal steps. "With your permission, of course. It will be your task to take care of unfinished business, arrange for the house to be sold, cash in the bonds, and eventually take charge of carving up the estate in equal amounts for the living relatives."

"I'm sorry," Frieda said. "You should probably run through that again for my husband. It's all a jumble in my head."

Eddie told him that his own father, Hugh's only brother, had long ago predeceased him. "That means it'll have to be divided amongst the rest of us." There were eleven boys in the family once, and one sister, an even dozen. "Some of us are gone, but most left kids behind. Shouldn't be too hard to figure out the arithmetic." He paused, then added, "I guess your fee will come off the top."

Frieda took the telephone receiver back. "There's no record anywhere that he intended to pay for our airfare?"

"Not that I'm aware of, Mrs. Macken."

"And you think we need to fly to Ottawa again?" The wall calendar had been changed – a photo of red boats in Peggy's Cove – but she couldn't recall doing it herself.

"I suppose it isn't absolutely necessary, but I think it would be much less complicated if you did. For instance, there is the matter of the house, which will have to be readied for sale. The contents dealt with."

"Couldn't we hire people?"

"Hired people could not be relied upon to watch out for any legal papers there might be in the house, or perhaps another will that has been overlooked, or records of investments."

"I see. I don't suppose we'd better waste any time then."

When she'd put the phone down, Eddie said, "You're flitting off to Ottawa again? Your back must be cured!"

"My back's killing me, but we can't give that woman time to think up some way of getting back what she thought she had. I'll lay down in the airplane aisle if I have to. I'll ship myself in a box. There's no way I can get out of going this time. We'll have to miss out on Bill Ireland's retirement party."

"It isn't his retirement party," Eddie said.

Frieda laughed. "I meant his birthday."

"It isn't his birthday," Eddie said. "It's his funeral."

Frieda sat in the nearest chair.

"Did you get it straight what that fellow was telling you?" Eddie said. "He's *our* lawyer now. The family's. You know what's going to happen?"

"Yes!" This, she could be sure of. "I just needed a minute to sort out my head. It's simple. Everybody gets the same amount in the end, but I do all the work."

VI

Fortunately a Mrs. Desjardins in the duplex next-door had a key and claimed to know exactly who they were, having seen them coming and going on their previous visit. Mr. Macken had mentioned them favourably to her as well. She was very sorry to hear of the old man's passing, she said, she hadn't known him well but they'd spoken over the fence. She looked at the suitcases in their hand and expressed surprise. "I didn't think you would want to stay in the house."

Frieda was embarrassed to be seen with these hideous things. "Oh my gosh, we don't! Our luggage is at the hotel."

"These were his," Eddie quickly said. "He gave them to us but we brought them back."

Frieda was grateful to see that the neighbour's friendly face did not betray any sign of having heard of luggage thieves. She handed over the key and stood watching from her open doorway as they crossed the grass to Uncle Hugh's front yard.

With a little luck they would never have to meet the Thorpe woman. In Frieda's imagination she was a four-hundred-pound giantess with hairy legs as thick as milk cans. She would fill the doorway with her bulk, and screw up one eye in order to direct hate-filled glances out of the other.

This would not be the first time they had cleaned out the house of a deceased bachelor. For years in advance the whole family had joked about the dreaded job of cleaning out dirty old Great-Uncle Bert's shack when the time came. They knew the task would require shovels, the dirt and grease were so thick. There was also the smell of the cat that had died behind the stove. It was suggested that someone put a match to the place, but of course they scrubbed it spotless so that the realtors could show it to potential buyers who would demolish it as soon as they'd signed the papers.

Eddie had mentioned the boys, thinking that maybe they should be told their reason for flying to Ottawa again, but she had objected. "They'd feel they should offer to help."

"And what's so terrible about that?"

"I don't want them to worry!" Her voice had gone a little too high. "I hope we've got a ways to go yet before we're completely useless." She'd seen how quickly others had been deprived of their independence. Olive Rennie's son had thrown her into a home the first time she forgot to turn off her electric stove.

A shiver passed through her as she stepped in through Uncle Hugh's doorway. She was invading his world, yet would not get to see his dear old face.

It didn't take long to see that someone had removed the dishwashers. Someone had also removed the washing machines, the refrigerators, and the television sets. They had not removed stacks of newspapers, or cardboard boxes, or old tattered furniture, however. Nor had they washed walls or cleaned dust from the corners. Where the house had looked overcrowded and junky before, it could now be described as simply a filthy mess. Rags and papers had been kicked around. Ropes of oily dust hung from the ceiling. Old stuffed chairs and chesterfield were littered with plastic bags and spilled cartons of empty bottles. Frieda Macken felt as though she'd been blindsided and left panting. "Ransacked!"

Eddie said, "Son of a bitch," and kicked a newspaper out from under his shoe.

Because the telephone had been disconnected, Frieda crossed the front lawn and asked with trembling voice if she might use Mrs. Desjardin's phone. The lawyer, when he was informed that the house had been plundered, asked if she had noticed signs of a break-in. There were other keys in existence, after all.

"I understand," Frieda said. She put down the phone and examined her hands while she sorted out her thoughts. It meant getting ahold of herself, pushing the confusion and anger aside. Think! Think! Don't let your brain turn to mush! Her gaze searched Mrs. Desjardin's kitchen for inspiration, but her thoughts lost their way for a moment as they registered counters as clean and tidy as her own. Why was she surprised? One fridge. One stove. One dishwasher. A chrome electric kettle reflected her white hair. She grabbed up Mrs. Desjardins' telephone book and found the Thorpes' number.

Mrs. Thorpe's voice expressed puzzlement. "I don't understand what you mean? What is missing?"

"Dishwashers are missing," Frieda said. "Washing machines are missing. Toasters. Television sets. One of the refrigerators is missing."

"They are not missing at all!" The woman's pleasant voice caught in a little laugh. "They are here! He insisted on giving them to us! As gifts."

"Which means," Frieda said, "that you now have three washing machines? Two or three dishwashers. Two new blenders. And God knows how many toasters! Your house must be awfully crowded."

When she returned to Uncle Hugh's house, Eddie was sitting on the front porch step. "Both fiddles are gone," he said.

She sat beside him, the sudden drop forcing a noisy gust of air from her lungs. Despite this late-spring sunshine, the concrete was a chill beneath her. "She says he gave everything to her." Every bone in her feet hurt, every muscle in her back. "I just bet he did!"

"You'll never prove he didn't." With his elbows on his knees and his hands under his jaw, he watched a large blue van pass by. The glass was the kind you couldn't see through, even if you got behind one and needed to see what a traffic light was doing up ahead. He hated those things, she knew. He thought there ought to be a law against tinted glass in vehicles. "Did you ask her why she accused us of being thieves?"

"I didn't think of it." She looked out across the street, where a tree she did not know the name of was in bloom.

Two small children came down the sidewalk, probably walking home from school for their lunch. The little girl waved. Frieda and Eddie waved back. "Where you goin'?" Eddie called.

The girl said something that sounded French. Eddie, grinning, shook his head. "Mercy beau-coo!" Both children squealed, and ran.

Inside the one refrigerator that had been left behind, mould grew on jars of jam. Cabbages and carrots were wet and black, and fell apart in Frieda's hand. Patterns of dark growth had spread across the interior walls. Too lazy to clean it out, the thieves had left it behind. She shut the door. "I can't face it yet."

She said the same about the mess in the living room. She said the same about the guest room, and the bathroom, too – mould growing on the walls. She felt the weight of the entire house on her shoulders. What had made them think they could do this themselves? Anybody with any brains would have hired someone. But of course, there were those missing papers to think about.

Jobs like this would not have stymied them in the past. They'd always known exactly where to start, how to go about it. Cleaning out Uncle Bert's mess had turned into a family party. But there was no fun in doing this alone.

"If we just walked away and left it?" she suggested.

He looked at her as if she'd suggested torching the place. Of course he was right to be shocked. She decided to open the Thermos of coffee while they thought about how to go about this job. But Eddie could not settle long. "That mess is not going away by itself. You can sit there if you want, but I'm gonna make a start."

All at once the front step was a foreign place she didn't want to be. "Well, you're not doing it alone!" She made a show of emptying the mugs back into the Thermos.

In the living room she opened out a plastic garbage bag and tossed in a *Saturday Evening Post.* 1958. Eddie bent and gathered up an armful of old newspapers and pushed them down. "The first thing we ought to do is get rid of them suitcases," he said. "The neighbour saw we brought them back, now we can take them out and burn them."

"We cannot," Frieda said a little too harshly. "If anyone comes to check out the house, I want them sitting in the middle of the living room floor." She took hold of them herself and placed them, for the time being, on the raised fireplace hearth, one beside the other in front of the heaped-up ashes.

They worked in silence, to clear the rooms of obvious garbage first. Newspapers. Magazines. Shoeboxes. Worn slippers. Broken irons. Tubes of toothpaste. As each bag was filled, Frieda closed it with a twist tie and Eddie carried it outside to stack with the others in the yard. She could see no point in talking about it.

Two, three hours went by in this manner. Once floors were cleared of everything but carpets and furniture, she devoted herself to kitchen cupboards. This was something familiar. How many times had she cleaned a kitchen cupboard in her life? Only a few of the dishes were worth keeping – she stacked them in cartons. Cereal boxes, half-empty bags of sugar, sticky bottles of maple syrup all went into the garbage bags. She'd be here forever if she started imagining this sort of thing was worth keeping.

She would have kept some of it herself if she'd lived nearby, but she was certainly not going to haul it onto a plane. Anyway someone – Kitty – might discover she'd kept a few ounces of sugar without sharing it with the others, without dividing it a dozen ways.

What she ought to do was take something – the maple syrup, the ketchup – and divide it into twelve equal portions in little Ziploc bags, and pass them out when she got home. This was the sort of thing she would have done once. This was the sort of thing they'd once expected of her. The rest of them would drag out the bathroom scales and make a big thing of comparing, to make sure they had all been given exactly the same amount. They would have worked it up into an evening's entertainment. They would joke about calling the local paper, to have a photographer sent out to take their photos holding their little transparent bags: Showing off the Inheritance.

She couldn't risk that now. What would once have been a happy form of self-mockery could now be something genuine and ugly. She retrieved the fullest bag of sugar from the garbage bag, and the heaviest boxes of cereal, and lined them up on the counter for Mrs. Desjardins. The box of salt had not been opened.

For lunch they sat on living-room chairs whose cushions hadn't seen the light of day in years, and ate from the carton of items they'd bought at a delicatessen across from the hotel. She closed her eyes. It was only when you stopped moving that you noticed how painful a back could be. She nibbled at ham slices but left the bread,, which was dry and tasteless.

"I'm dreading that fridge," she eventually said, "but we can't just throw it away! There'll be poor people glad to have it." She made an effort to rise, but fell back. "I can't face it." But she heaved herself upright anyway, to avoid seizing up altogether. "First I'm going to scrub that filthy bathroom within an inch of its life."

She saw herself – her own tired face, her wildly messed-up hair, her saddened eyes looking back from the dusty mirror above the two hideous suitcases. She snatched her gaze away.

The afternoon passed. Eventually, the bathroom walls and ceiling smelled of disinfectant. The bathtub shone. The medicine cabinet, stripped clean, was Windexed free of dirt, Lysoled free of germs. The sink and taps gleamed. There was nothing she could do about the chip in the sink. There was nothing she could do about the torn shower curtain either, except yank it down and push it into one of the large green garbage bags.

She did not do any of this at home any more, she hadn't done this sort of thing since her back had started acting up. The housecleaner had instructions to get the place so clean you could eat off the floors. Of course it was never quite as she would have done it herself, so she ran the vacuum cleaner over the heavy-traffic spots before company arrived. Now, wedged between Uncle Hugh's toilet and the wall, she reached to scrape out gunk from the baseboard corners. "Oh, I can't stand it!" she cried out, without intending to. The first human voice in the house for two or three hours. Something of a wail.

Eddie appeared at the door, a shoebox in his hand. "Something here the battleaxe overlooked."

Frieda got to her feet, or tried to. "What is it?" Before going through all the effort of straightening her back, she'd wait to see if it was worth it.

"Savings Bonds. Not much. A few hundred dollars."

Frieda stood up to look at the sheets of paper – fold lines worn across them. "His signature – old-fashioned handwriting. He must have had the same teacher as my dad."

"Keep your eyes open," he said. "This was in a box of snapshots. Old bugger's liable to have others where you least expect it."

"I don't care any more how much there is. If I'm going to break my neck cleaning this mess I can only do it if I'm doing it for him."

"You're not doing it for him," Eddie said.

Her chin came up. "I am so." She looked at a pair of plaster ducks flying up the wall and snatched them from their flight. She flashed her eyes at him, and shoved the painted ducks down amongst the wadded-up paper towels. The ugly things would be as old as the house.

"You're doing it for your father." He could thrust out his jaw as well as she could, with his infuriating grin.

She turned away. If they couldn't talk without raising their voices she might as well get on with the job in silence.

They had to come back the following day, and the next as well, before the house began to look presentable. Several containers of Old Dutch Cleanser were emptied. Two boxes of Spic and Span. Twice they had to replace the sponge attachment to the mop handle. The garbage bags, standing side by side, nearly filled the backyard. They stopped for a rest every thirty minutes now. Aching backs were never mentioned. Frieda didn't even bother trying to stand up straight, she would wait until she could be sure she wouldn't have to get down on her knees again.

Down on her knees with a paring knife, a Jet pad, a scrubbing brush, and a pail of soapy water. There was no other way to get corners. "Serves me right, I guess, for joking about that mansion. This is one way to eat humble pie!"

"In fifty years I haven't seen you eat it yet. You'll find a way of calling it Baked Alaska."

"If they'd thrown us in jail for stealing those suitcases I'd be lying in my cell right now, reading books while someone cooks my supper. I'm pretty sure they wouldn't make a woman my age scrub floors."

"Just keep in mind that every spot you clean is upping the price – putting a few more pennies in my relatives' pockets."

While they sat on the front step with their coffee, the neighbour came across the adjoining lawns. "You have been working too hard, I think." There was a slight accent in her speech. No "h" – *t'ink* instead of *think*, *'ave* instead of *have*. She seemed worried. Did they look so bad?

"Something to drink?" Eddie said. "We have coffee in that Thermos. Coffee substitute in this one here. Ice water over there. I already drank the beer."

Mrs. Desjardins waved the offer away. She was a heavy woman, middle-aged, wearing a loose denim blouse. She had been wondering, she said, what they would do with what had not been stolen. "Beds. Chairs. Tables, if there are any."

"We don't want to hang around long enough to have a yard sale," Eddie said. "Better just let someone come in and take the whole damn works away."

"That is what I thought," said Mrs. Desjardins. "My son, he says he would be happy to manage a yard sale and send you the money. He was fond of your uncle."

Frieda sighed her relief. "We could offer you one of his new washing machines for your trouble, but they seem to have run away."

Mrs. Desjardins smiled. "My son, I think he would be happy to have a chair or two, or a couch, for his basement room."

"You know this Mrs. Thorpe?" Eddie said.

The woman's smile disappeared. "Well. I have seen her, of course, coming in and out. The poor old men, they don't know any better than to be grateful, eh? She make friends with them in their own homes first, then she offer to take them in when they need it. What can you do?"

"My gosh," Frieda said when Mrs. Desjardins had returned to her house. "This scares me half to death. Don't you go dying and leaving me behind."

"What are you talking about? You've got children. Grand-children. Who would try to take advantage of you?"

"There'll be something we never heard of. We'd never heard of this sort of thing, had we? I think I'd rather jump off a bridge."

"Don't get started. When the time comes, you won't even care. So long as they feed you and put a roof over your head."

"And don't hit you. You read about that too."

"Your own children could do that."

"Don't say that!" She stood up, though it took time, and turned, with a fist to the small of her back, to go into the house. "I just hope your family appreciates this."

"They won't thank you for it," he said. "They'll wonder why we didn't ask them to help."

⁂

The old refrigerator could not be put off any longer. Frieda got down on her knees and started to take things out. Rotted vegeta-bles, mouldy jars, unrecognizable blobs of leftover meat. A bucket of soapy hot water made a start. Then Jet pads and spray cleaners and Comet were put to work.

"Let's see," she called – down on her knees with her head in the fridge. "We'll probably get something like fifty dollars for this stupid fridge. Divided a dozen ways, that's four dollars each. That's two dollars an hour I'll get for my trouble!"

Eddie had the kitchen tap apart, examining the worn washer. If he were home, he'd have washers in the basement to replace it. Here, he would have to go out to a store. "What do you mean *you* get? You don't get a cent out of this. The four dollars comes to me. After the lawyer's got his share. The fact is, you don't get nothing at all yourself."

"That's right!" Her voice echoed inside. "And you'll probably bonk me on the head and spend it on some young blonde." She sat back on the floor. "That's going to have to do." It had taken nearly two hours but she had it spotless, gleaming, radiantly clean. She, on the other hand, was a mess – gritty, sweaty, smudged, in need of a bath. "I can't stand this any longer. I don't know if I can get up."

He left the sink and came closer. "You want a hand?"

She twisted her face, made an effort to get to her feet. "This is ridiculous." She tried to laugh. "Just shove me back in the fridge and close the door. Use it for my coffin."

"You'd like that, wouldn't you? Pall bearers hauling that thing to the cemetery."

"Well, it makes sense!" she said. "God knows I spent my life in the kitchen, I must've opened a fridge door twenty times a day."

"Nora'd say you did it out of spite. Cheating her out of her fridge to save the price of a coffin."

"I may start a trend. Housewives taking their refrigerators with them. Kitty'd have to be crammed inside her guitar."

"Now you're getting stupid. Give me your hand." His large callused hand reached down and waited.

"Well, she's almost small enough! Grab under this arm."

He did, but rearranged his feet for stronger purchase. "Wait a
minute now, let me park myself against this wall. I don't want to
end up down there with you."

With one of his hands beneath the top of her arm, she grunted
and strained upwards, and came eventually to her feet. Smiling,
she patted his shoulder and pulled his head down to kiss him on
the lips. "Isn't it fun getting old?"

He shook his head and raised his eyes, as if there were someone
else in the room to see. "With you around, it sure as hell don't
have a chance to get dull."

VII

She thought the knock at the door might be room service.
They'd been too tired to dress and go down to the dining room for
dinner. But it wasn't anyone connected to the hotel. A middle-
aged couple stood back from the door, both smiling. The woman
was a little taller than the man, wider too. Both wore lengthy
overcoats of some lightweight grey material.

"Mrs. Macken?" the woman said. Her pale hair was pulled
back severely from her face, and largely hidden inside a pink cro-
cheted hat. She tilted her head to the side in a sort of coquettish
way that did not suit her.

She was Mrs. Thorpe, she said. This was Mr. Thorpe. The little
man smiled. His nod was very nearly a bow. They wondered if

they might come in for a moment, the woman said, they had something they wished to discuss.

Eddie's frown deepened. No handshakes were offered on either side. Frieda felt a chill in her arms, a tightening in her chest. She had hoped to escape a confrontation, she'd thought they would get home without even meeting this woman. Now, almost without realizing what she was doing, she'd gone and invited her into their room. But of course she'd never turned anyone away in her life.

"We were pleased to hear that you'd come," said Mrs. Thorpe. "We had been thinking of making a trip to the Coast in order to talk with you."

The Thorpes each sat in a chair before chairs had been offered. Frieda did not suggest they remove their coats, though it was warm in the room. They hadn't yet figured out how to control the temperature, and the windows wouldn't open. Frieda sat in a short couch against the wall. Eddie sat down beside her. As soon as they'd settled, the visitors pulled their chairs up so close that the four pairs of knees were all but touching one another.

"We wish to make a proposal," the woman said in a lowered voice, as though she feared being overheard by neighbours.

"We're tired," Eddie said. "We spent the day on our hands and knees scrubbing floors."

"You shouldn't be doing that," Mr. Thorpe said, at though she were speaking to frail children. "You should have hired some boy to do it. Or left it." His face was broad and flat and bland.

"Left it?" Frieda said. "We had to clear out the junk to see if anything worthwhile had been overlooked by the people who ransacked the place." She punched down a cushion and wedged it between herself and the arm of the uncomfortable couch. Rough tan-coloured serge. Everything in this room was the colour of mud. Not a shiny thing in sight. You couldn't tell if anything was clean.

The Thorpes waited, as though there was something more they expected to hear.

"I'm sorry," Frieda said when the cushion was firmly in place. "But this whole business has upset me more than you could know." She cast a second cushion onto her lap, and then pummelled it into shape for use on the other side. "I think it's a terrible thing you did to my uncle." Her tone sounded so foreign to her own ears that she laughed.

"That is not what we came to speak about," said Mrs. Thorpe. "We have considered it carefully, and have taken what we know would be Mr. Macken's wishes into consideration." She spoke carefully, as though she had come to English late, or was making an effort to remain unexcited. Perhaps she believed she was addressing idiots. Pink spots the size of dimes had appeared in her cheeks. "Mr. Macken made it clear, you see, that he wished everything to be left to us."

It wasn't unusual for Frieda to discover she liked someone she'd expected not to like at all. She just naturally liked people, once she'd met them and saw how *real* they were. But there was no chance of that happening this time. This woman had *cornered* her here, something that would never have happened if she'd entered Frieda's house.

"Show us where it's written down," Eddie said.

"He was not well enough to complete that business," said Mrs. Thorpe. Her hands lay curled one inside the other on her lap. "Nevertheless he was clear about his wishes. But that is also not what we have come here to say. We have come here to say that we will be happy to put Mr. Macken's wishes aside to a certain extent, and to make a proposal. We will not challenge your right to the money – whatever bonds or investment money he owned – in exchange for the house."

"I don't understand what you're saying," Frieda said. "Eddie?"

"She's saying they want the house," Eddie said, as though he were irritated with Frieda rather than Mrs. Thorpe. "It's a kind of a threat."

Mrs. Thorpe smiled, showing slightly crooked teeth. "Of course it is not a threat." She leaned forward just a little over her hands, which had remained laced together at her waist but were starting to show signs of agitation. Fingers opened and closed.

Eddie stood up and pushed past the barrier of knees. "She's saying that having stripped the house of everything in it, including a $70,000 violin, she wants to have the house itself as well." Finding a package of Players in a jacket pocket, he set about getting one lit. "While we are welcome to whatever papers we uncovered while we were cleaning up the mess she left. Papers she overlooked."

"It is only reasonable," Mrs. Thorpe said. She looked at Frieda now, since Eddie had removed himself. "When you consider his wish that we have everything. He was not ungrateful for the care he was given in our home."

"I'm sure he wasn't," Frieda said. Pinned to the wall and deserted, she might as well be blunt. "I'm sure he never saw my letters either. I'm sure he was never told about the phone calls."

"I don't remember any letters," said Mrs. Thorpe. "We were surprised to learn that he had relatives, he spoke as though he were all alone in the world. Until, of course, he mentioned the suitcases. Even then, he did not admit that there was any blood relationship."

"I think you should leave," said Eddie from behind the pair of intruders. "If we have anything to say to one another it should be in front of a lawyer."

"It is a simple matter," said Mrs. Thorpe, showing no sign that she'd heard. Her hands were separated now, her fingers busy with the folds in her coat. "We wish to keep the house. We will allow you to keep whatever bonds there might be. And then, of course, no charges will be laid."

"Charges!" Frieda cried. This was so unforeseen that she wasn't sure she hadn't laughed. She whipped out one of cushions from beside her and slapped it down on her lap.

"Two suitcases," said Mr. Thorpe. "Two suitcases that the poor old man said you took from his home."

"He *gave* them to us!" Frieda said. Her hated the sound of her own voice when it went shrill. She reined it in. Lowered her chin. "He gave the stupid things to us, we didn't even want them! Eddie?"

"Easy now," Eddie said. He pushed in past the knees and rejoined her on the couch, holding an amber ashtray that could in a pinch become a weapon. It occurred to Frieda how unreal this must seem for him, after a life in the woods. But then, it was every bit as foreign to her. They were country people up against a world they'd never imagined.

"That may very well be the case," said Mr. Thorpe. Though his eyes moved from one to the other of the culprits, his head had remained rigid on his neck since he'd arrived. "Nevertheless, whatever the outcome, we will have the opportunity to repeat what he told us, for the benefit of the authorities."

"Whether you took them illegally or not," said Mrs. Thorpe, "if news of it gets around there will be some who wonder what was *in* those cases. We offer you a way of avoiding this unpleasantness."

"I don't believe my ears," Frieda said, looking this way and that, as if someone might be found to correct what she'd just heard. She felt as though her body had taken on several hundred pounds of extra weight, all of it giving in to the insistent pull of gravity.

"I think we've heard just about enough," Eddie said, standing again. "You'd better get out of here."

The Thorpes did not get to their feet. "It is a reasonable offer," said Mrs. Thorpe. "You may keep whatever is in the bank. We are asking only that you allow us to keep the house, which we feel we have earned. After all, I kept food in his stomach when he was too ill to look after himself. And made sure he took his medicine at the correct time. I kept an eye on him so that he would not wander out into the traffic and get himself run over by a truck."

Frieda thought of the strangers who'd brought her father home from the dike road. "Of course you're right about that," she said. She started at the sound of her own words. "What am I saying? You raided his bank accounts. You cashed his pension cheques. You made sure you were rewarded with every penny you could get your hands on. Then, once he'd conveniently died, you took everything that was worth anything out of his house. You're just mad because you didn't get to steal the house as well."

The woman had closed her eyes while she waited for Frieda to finish, as if to suggest that she couldn't bear the sight of anyone who would make such preposterous accusations. Then she continued as though she had closed off her ears as well. "When he fell and could not get up for three days, he would have died if I hadn't come knocking on his door. His life was extended by several months because of us. A little two-bedroom house is not too much of a reward for that. Your good name will be untouched by gossip."

Frieda put a hand to her head. "Oh, they're confusing me!" What had seemed so clear was no longer clear at all. She felt like a child, a young girl being scolded for something she hadn't even known she'd done. "I don't know what to think."

"You don't need to think," Eddie said. "These people are leaving. We've got nothing to say to them."

"Are you sure?" Frieda said. She was frightened now. Her hands were giving the cushion in her lap a good wringing. "I hate it when things aren't clear."

"It is a sensible business proposition," said Mr. Thorpe.

"They'll charge us with theft if we don't let them keep the house," Eddie translated. He crossed the room and opened the door to the hallway. "They've forgotten that since the old man didn't leave a will them suitcases belong to us. They think seeing our names in the paper is enough to scare a couple of stupid hicks. I don't think it is. What do you think?"

Frieda bowed her head, rested her forehead on her hand. "I think I must be losing my mind. To sit here and listen to this! Nobody's ever treated us like this before."

"If you'd come around saying this sort of thing a few years ago," Eddie said, taking hold of Mr. Thorpe's arm and starting to raise him from his seat, "you'd find yourself tossed out on the road. By God I'll boot you down the stairwell if you don't get out on your own."

"We must've been a sight," Frieda would later report to the relatives. "Two old crippled-up fogeys pushing those two from

the room. Both of them still talking! Eddie had no trouble drag-
ging that little runt to the door, but here I was with both hands
out in front like this, pushing that woman's shoulders like she was
a mule that wouldn't budge. Still telling me we ought to do the
sensible thing."

In the end, the husband had taken his wife's hand and led her
out. Before slamming the door, Eddie said, "The suitcases were
never stolen. We found them yesterday, under all the junk in his
house. You could've found them yourself while you were robbing
the place if you had any eyes in your heads. They're sitting in
front of the fireplace now where nobody can miss them."

"I broke a nail on that woman's coat," Frieda told the others.
"My glasses were knocked to the floor. Trying to shove that big
lump out the door while I was practically blind! Too bad I didn't
push her out the window by mistake."

"Did I just hear that Eddie Macken told a lie?" Buddy Macken
said. "I never heard him lie before in his life. Is this what happens
when we let you run off to the city?"

Buddy and Grace had stopped in on their way home from the
chiropractor. Outside, the heavy sky had lowered to somewhere
just above the Douglas firs, the dark world streaked by steady
drizzle. Inside, the ceiling light was reflected only dimly in the
retirement silver set – which, Frieda noticed only now, had small
dark spots of tarnish here and there, though she had wrapped it
in clear plastic before they'd gone east. After her cataract operation she hoped to catch these things much sooner.

"Just a little white lie," she said. "But he paid for it. He tossed
all night, he couldn't sleep. I told him it didn't matter. Well, my
gosh! But it nearly drove him crazy that he'd lied so easy. He'd be
brooding about it even now if something else hadn't happened."

Grace put down her cup and leaned forward. "The police?"

"I thought it might be," Frieda said. "Next morning he was in the shower when there was a knock on the door." She paused, recalling the sound. She imagined police with a warrant. Or a warning at least. "I was scared to open it, expecting to be dragged away in handcuffs." She bit into her piece of Grace's square and waited until she had chewed and swallowed. "But – it was that little man again! Her husband! I slammed the door in his face and hollered for Eddie. He came out with a towel around his waist, soaking wet, hollering 'What? What?' like he thought I was being murdered." She laughed, remembering the look on Eddie's face, his hands grappling with the towel to keep it from slipping. "And now there's another knock, *bang bang bang*. But he waits until he's stepped into his pants to open it."

"I told him he wasn't coming in this time," Eddie said, getting up and going into the kitchen for the coffee pot. "But he didn't want to, he just holds out his hand like this." He went around the table refilling cups. "'Our key to the house,' he says, and drops it into my hand. 'We won't bother you no more.' Then he turns and goes away."

"Ashamed," Grace said. "You'd like to think so, anyway. Once he seen them honest faces he knew they'd made a mistake – tried to bully *decency*."

"I think he just wanted us to know it wasn't his idea." Frieda said. "That woman must've cooked the whole thing up and forced him to go along. Anyway, before he got back to the elevator – no surprise in this – Honest Eddie here goes after him, with his bare chest still soaking wet and dripping soap bubbles on the carpet. He told him –"

"I told him we didn't find the luggage in the house like I said," Eddie said. "I told him we only had it because Uncle Hugh forced us to take it." While Grace and Buddy laughed, he returned the coffee pot to the stove and came back to sit at the head of the dining-room table. Frieda shot him a "thank you" look. She was too sore to get up and pour the coffee herself, every muscle in her body aching, every bone a catalogue of bruises.

Rain fell. Cars raced by on the highway in a spray of their own making, their weak headlights smearing pale smudges across the day. The drivers didn't even know they were crossing lawn – or once-was lawn, sacrificed in order to straighten out a corner.

Grace shook her head. "You weren't scared enough to consider their offer?" You could tell she hoped they had been. Or might be yet. "Even for a minute or two?" She'd brought the plate of date squares they were eating. Frieda hadn't had time to bake since getting home, nor had she thought to thaw something from her freezer.

"I was scared," Frieda admitted. "But giving in to them never entered my head. I don't know if Eddie –"

Eddie snorted contempt at the very idea. "The worst they coulda done is get our names in the paper. Without that new will, nothing belongs to them. If I coulda seen a sliver of *right* on their side –"

"They'll find more old men to sucker in," Buddy gravely said. He tipped up his cup and drained it. When he'd returned his cup to his saucer he said, "I'd like to've seen the two of you pushing them out the door. That must've been a sight."

"Don't encourage them," Grace said. "They'll start acting it out."

Frieda laughed. "For a while there I thought you'd be sending care packages to an Ottawa jail cell. For all we know, Ontario cops put luggage-theft up there with robbing the Mint!"

While his eyes followed a cyclist passing by on the highway, head down against the rain, Buddy spoke as though this were only a matter of casual interest: "I wonder what your boys'd say if you had to call them from prison."

It seemed that every nerve in Frieda's body reacted to this. "There's no need for them to hear!" It hadn't occurred to her that she would have this to worry about. "Not all of it, anyway." Perhaps, as a tale of adventure one day. "My gosh! There's no sense in getting them upset."

Eddie grinned. Of course he would know what she was thinking: No sense letting them get it into their heads to start keeping an eye on us.

"God knows what Kitty will make of it," Grace said. "A country-and-western opera at the least!"

Frieda said nothing to that. Licking her index finger, she used it to pick up the scattered rolled oats that had fallen from her piece of square. Grace was so afraid of soggy middles that she overcooked everything. Sawdust in your mouth. *Act it out?* They weren't likely to see her acting it out. Not until it had got so far behind them, so often retold, that it was just another adventure.

"And you really took them suitcases back?" Grace said. She sounded disappointed.

"My gosh, I *hope* we did!" Frieda said. "I don't know what's going on in my stupid head, but every time I come round that hallway corner there I expect to see them. Sometimes I've gone right past and think I *have* seen them and have to go back to make sure they aren't there." She threw out her hands as though to suggest they might as well haul her away right now and shoot her. Then, because all at once she was tired of this, she put both hands on the table as though she were about to stand.

"You okay?" Eddie said.

"Tired," Grace answered for her. "This exciting life must be exhausting."

"And Eddie's anxious to get back to his chainsaw," Frieda said. "He's been home for twenty-four hours and hasn't felled a single tree."

"I have," Eddie said. He'd made himself sound indignant and amused, but she could sense embarrassment. "One tall balsam fir. Thirty minutes is all I had before you come out to see where I'd got to."

He was right. A grey flannel screen peeled back from in front of this morning. She'd gone out looking for him, she'd found him in the shadowed timber amongst the salal, knee-deep in the blue exhaust from his noisy saw. His red hard hat, his thick wool Stanfield shirt. He was bending forward, with one foot up on the fallen tree, while he lopped off one and then another of its limbs. The stray cat watched from a nearby stump.

She laughed. What else could she do? She leapt to her feet and hobbled to the kitchen with her cup and saucer and put them in the sink. Then she leaned against the counter and turned on the tap and squirted liquid soap. What was she doing? She turned off the tap. Washing dishes while the others were still at the table! She went back to join them and dropped into her chair. "All this travel has scrambled my brains! You better make sure I stay put until my old self catches up to me again."

ASTONISHING THE BLIND

I should have been practising this afternoon, I should be getting dressed and ready to walk to the concert hall, but I have been sitting here for most of an hour by the phone, unable to pick it up. You'll have some explaining to do, I'm afraid, when you are asked if "the daughter who lives in Europe" has called. How will you explain that I haven't? You may not get this letter for a week.

The clock in the *Markt Platz* should be striking six any moment. Above it a rooster will crow; beside it a guard will blow his horn and Death turn his hourglass over again. Of course I won't hear or see this from my desk at the guest-house window, but I've been to this town before and can imagine all this activity whenever a glance at my watch coincides with the hour. Church bells clang all over town, slamming metal against metal like wild children competing with pots and pans.

Carl will assume that I've called. You remain something of a hero to him, though it's been three years since you were together, where you could encourage one another's outrageous opinions. If he were here, he would pick up the telephone, even dial the numbers for me, and hold the receiver to my ear. "Your father," he would announce with pleasure, as though he had conjured you up.

But Carl did not come with me this time, though it is just a three-hour drive from our home. He travels enough already with his Euro-bureaucracy work.

Besides, he despises this town. He dislikes most of the towns in his country, even the one where we live, but he dislikes this one the most thoroughly because it is here that he was a student. He disapproves of the renewed popularity of fraternity houses, sponsored by leading citizens, with their rituals and fencing duels and their patriotic songs that make your blood run cold. He is convinced there are professors here, happily retired and still unpunished, who once practised "German physics" in the name of science. He finds it amusing that his alma mater is playing host to his wife, putting her up in this comfortable guest house and allowing her to perform in the beautiful old hall, the *alte aula*, surrounded by famous murals. I have instructions not to let it go to my head.

Perhaps I already have. I wish you could see the room where I performed last evening and will again tonight, the grand hall in the original university building. Chandeliers hang from a ceiling where crossbeams have been decorated with hand-painted figures. Giant Gothic windows fill one wall with stained-glass circle patterns. And wide paintings decorate the other walls with the city's history. The audience sees, at my back, a file of indignant Dominican monks leaving the city, expelled by a prince who has decided to erect the world's first Protestant university on the very spot their monastery has occupied for centuries. The first professors taught their heresies from precisely where the piano and I challenge conventional approaches to Mozart.

I'd forgotten something Carl had told me about this town — that this is where the blind come from all over the country to be trained, so that they can get around and do everything the same as everyone else. This did not occur to me until I was standing at an intersection yesterday afternoon, waiting for a traffic light to change. All at once I saw that there were blind people every-where I looked – not in groups or clusters, but all going in various directions at various speeds. I am in a city of the blind, I thought. I almost said it aloud, liking the notion, as if there were some-thing magical about it. It was startling to see how quickly they moved, with their white canes swinging back and forth before them without quite touching the ground – electronic in some way, I imagine, like the sonar system of bats. They walked faster than I, some of them, and with far more confidence. Nothing tentative, nothing apologetic about them. I saw one young woman run to catch a bus that was about to pull away. Almost immediately afterwards, a tall man came from behind and skipped carefully around me in his hurry to cross the street.

Not surprisingly, there were quite a few of the blind in my audience last evening. I found myself grateful to them for coming, though this was silly, of course, since you don't need eyesight in order to enjoy Rachmaninoff or my favourite Beethoven sonatas. It was just that I imagined them finding their way with confi-dence and speed, separately and from all over town, getting themselves through the foyer and down the long hallway to the grand old hall without help, and finding seats in the crowd. It occurred to me that they may have been trained to hear more critically, and more appreciatively, than anyone else in the room. I played in order to astonish them.

I can't see it from here, the old university building with that wonderful hall, though the view from this guest-house desk includes the castle at the top of the hill and a jumble of timbered, steep-roofed fairytale houses spilling down the slope. Immediately before me is the *alter botanischer garten* with its neglected flower beds. Wild mustard grows up through the roses. Its grass has gone to seed – some of it deliberately, I understand, for the birds. Its garbage cans are overturned, its pathways littered with the green dung of free-roaming swans.

This afternoon I walked out along the gravel pathways of this former botanical garden with my dear old teacher – you remember my speaking of Professor Mueller? – who arranged to be driven up from his retirement home so that he could hear me perform last night. He assured me that he'd been pleased with my performance. I think you would have been proud as well. Of course he noticed, and he let me know that he'd noticed, that I have not yet entirely mastered the art of risking originality – or rather, had not yet mastered it with confidence. I am still too North American, he says, after all these years – seventeen!

He must be in his eighties now. Like you, he walks with a cane to keep his balance. This may have been what prompted me to mention you, and to tell him that today, ten thousand miles away, you were about to celebrate your sixtieth wedding anniversary.

Tears came suddenly to his eyes. He lost his own wife years ago, I remember. A woman he'd adored. "Still together after sixty years!" he said. "A happy marriage, I hope."

"Very," I said on your behalf. "One of those lifelong romances we read about but don't often witness. My folks have been inseparable since they were children."

Inseparable was the word he repeated. In his mouth it was filled with wonder.

Of course, with that word between us, I was forced to consider the violence that can be done by time. What does it mean to be "still together" anyway? To be inseparable, as you know better than anyone else, does not after all exclude the possibility of physical separation.

I held the professor's arm as we passed along the shoreline of a pond, where mallards sunbathed amongst the tangled surface roots of a sawed-off trunk, and entered a shaded plantation of sturdy old trees. These are specimens from around the world, of course, yet they have grown together here for so long that they appear to belong in one another's company. Blue spruce and redwood cedars and acacias and a variety of pines. We had to guess at these, since they have been stripped of Latin or German names and given orange stencilled numbers on their trunks instead, like inmates in some prison camp. I suppose their identities are available only to scholars with access to a university filing cabinet.

"But, Meg, you must wish you were there!" said my Professor Mueller, referring again to your diamond anniversary. I assured him that you understood the difficulty, when I was so far away. "I fly home every August, and stay for the month. This year I can't afford to go twice."

"And the children?" he said.

"Always go with me. They're teenagers now, yet they start counting the days in June, excited about seeing their grandparents again."

"And Carl?" he said. His old eyebrows have become grey caterpillars riding his brow. It was he who had introduced me to Carl, you remember, after my debut concert – a tall loose-limbed young man who came backstage with an armload of cornflowers.

"Carl used to go with me," I told him. "But he hasn't always been free in the past few years."

"And is not with you here?"

I began to suspect that this was not Professor Mueller at all who was quizzing me, but you in disguise. "He works hard all week," I said. "His weekends are precious. He has his own commitments."

When we had left the gardens and were walking back to the professor's hotel along a paved footpath that runs between a stream and the fence surrounding a nursing home, we came upon a woman I recognized from last night. She'd sat in the second row, and smiled throughout my performance in that secretive way that suggests some private satisfaction no one else could possibly share.

She was not smiling now. Nor was she walking with the confidence and speed I have become accustomed to here. She poked nervously ahead of herself with her white stick, veering toward the edge of the pavement. When she found herself jabbing at grass, she stopped, and poked at everything around her, experimenting, in order to set herself back on course.

I asked if there was something wrong, if we could do something to help. She drew our attention to her cane, which had a sharp bend toward the bottom. "Someone running," she said. "Tripped over my cane and fell. We both fell."

There were smudges of dirt on the knees of her corduroy pants.

"Then he got up and gave it back to me and ran off!" she said. "Didn't even give me his name. If he had given his name, his insurance might pay for a new one. Now I'll have to pay for it myself and I can't afford it."

Her voice suggested that the entire world was at fault. But there was little I could do about it. Professor Mueller's walking stick had no more magic in it than her wounded one. I offered to see her to her destination but she declined. She would get there eventually, she said, though it was obvious that she felt impotent and angry, reduced to the state of someone tapping along in a nineteenth-century novel or an old black-and-white movie.

I suppose Carl would not have given up so easily. He would have insisted on accompanying the woman to the administration building, or the library, even if this annoyed her. He would have known who to call, where to make a report. He might have had advice for appealing to the guilty man's conscience – an ad in the paper, perhaps – whereas I have thought of such things only now.

And my dear professor, once we had rejected his walking stick as useless, had gone into a brooding silence, unable or unwilling to say anything at all, as blank and confused and helpless as the silent elderly patients we could see in their grassy pen behind the chain-link fence.

I think of these people as the *alter leute* when I see them through the back kitchen window of my guest-house rooms. Neglected grandfathers stare out from benches onto that quiet yard. Neglected grandmothers curl up on cots to receive the attentions of the sun. One bent man in a dark cardigan pushes a walker slowly past, nodding to those who sit with knees apart and eyes on the past, and later makes the return journey, nodding his greetings again to those who watch. It is a long building, six or seven storeys tall. There must be hundreds of residents who never come out. Only once in my three days here have I seen a white uniform amongst those who risk the fresh air. And only once have I seen a visitor – a young woman talking with a white-haired man, whose expression was one of silent puzzlement: Who are you, and why have you suddenly appeared to yatter at me like this? "Your daughter," I imagine her saying. "Don't you remember me? Did you think I'd forgotten you?"

"Dear God," Professor Mueller said. He was looking through the fence at a pale dumpling of a woman who had been tied to a chair with the long cloth belt off a housecoat. She seemed to be looking back at him. "Those of us who are loved," he said, "can hardly imagine how much we have to be grateful for!"

Who do you have? I wanted to ask. I recall no children. Was he thinking of his lost wife? Perhaps he meant grateful students who, unlike me, live close enough to pay attention. Or neighbours who have grown attached.

I know that if I were to dial this phone now you would answer before the first ring was completed, since at this time of day (mid-morning for you) you will be installed beside the phone in your leather chair, watching out the window for someone (Gerry, I imagine) to pick you up and drive you to the hospital. I hope he will have flowers, and a cake, and perhaps even a few balloons.

Mom will be in her wheelchair now, I suppose, looking out at the view of the bay. Someone will have washed and set her beautiful hair. I hope they've put her in the dress that matches her blue eyes. I'm sure they have tried to make her understand there are reasons to be happy today. If only it were possible to help her recall, even briefly, what she must have felt on her day as an excited bride! I should pick up this bloody instrument now, if only to remind you to take flowers. Thinking of such things was never one of your strengths. I wonder if you remember that it is the larger, gaudier, long-stemmed flowers she has always liked best. Tiger lilies, shasta daisies, spiky mandarin orange dahlias. I have wired flowers myself, but flowers will mean more when they are delivered by someone whose face is at least familiar.

I remember thinking, one day last August as I left her room ahead of you, "There's next to nothing left of her. She is being slowly taken from us." But when I looked back through the doorway, you were bent over her bed, in danger of toppling forward on top of her, but laughing, mock-complaining, "My God, you're mushy today, woman!" Both of her hands came up to bring your face down to hers for a kiss. Whatever else has been taken, she still knows who she loves in this world.

I will not phone the hospital. The last time I phoned I was told that she would have to be wakened, and for a conversation that would probably only confuse her. I knew that she wouldn't recognize my voice, and would have to pretend she knew who I was. Nor would she remember the conversation five minutes afterwards. While I, on the other hand, would be unable to think of anything else for the rest of the day.

Poor Professor Mueller worried about that blind woman all the way back to his hotel. "There must be something we might have done," he said, his great furry eyebrows tilting down with concern. He turned this way and that, as though searching for inspiration amongst the foyer furniture. "All three of us standing about, equally helpless! What good were *our* eyes when we were needed?" He decided to be amused by this, a little. "We were of no more use to her than those poor deserted souls behind that terrible fence."

Before we parted, he lifted my hand to his lips. When I promised to report the incident of the damaged walking stick to university authorities, he looked up with relief and, I think, surprise. Then, still holding my hand, he admonished me to risk failure tonight with a more European brand of confidence. He also asked me to pass on his good wishes to my parents. And of course, as well, to Carl.

Carl will be leaving the flat any moment now, to keep an appointment of his own. The day will have been spent in household chores, in writing business letters, shopping for items I have asked him to buy, and arranging for a sitter so that he may now step out with a sense of satisfaction to conduct his acts of betrayal.

They meet at the bridge. That's all I know. I don't even know which bridge, though I imagine it is where you enter town from the south. In my mind he waits at the north end of the wet grey concrete bridge, standing under his umbrella (it is almost certainly raining there, though perhaps I only wish for this), watching for her approach along the riverbank from where she lives.

I don't know where they will go. Perhaps they go back to her place, after a stroll through the park. Certainly not to our house. They will drive out into the country and stop at a café along the riverfront, I suppose. Or they will drive all the way to the city to attend the cinema, or perhaps a recital in the concert hall. Because they are known as colleagues who sometimes must travel together for their work, they believe they have no reason to be circumspect. Does he believe that my friends have no eyes?

So you see where I have brought myself with these thoughts, with these words that were meant to be a way of avoiding things. It should not be such a difficult thing to pick up the telephone and wish you a Happy Sixtieth Anniversary. Dressed up and ready to go, you won't have the patience for a long-winded news report on my life. Long-distance charges being what they are, you won't expect it. With a little skill and some self-control we should be able to get through this without either of us wondering aloud what we mean.

But I suppose I have waited too long, as I must have intended, and you've almost certainly left for your lunch at Extended Care.

I may mail this on my way to the concert hall, if I find a yellow post box on the route, or I may try again to telephone afterwards. In the meantime, when I play the Beethoven this evening it will be not only to offer consolation to the dispossessed monks on the wall but also to salute the patience and fidelity of a lifelong love as I have witnessed it. And of course to astonish the blind.